DEATH FROM THE DARKNESS

A muzzle flash stabbed out of the darkness between two buildings they'd just passed. Clint's arm instinctively tightened around Thelma and he drove her to the sidewalk, his right hand scooting for his six-gun. He heard a second shot strike the woman just as his gun came up and he fired into the shadows between buildings. He fired again and again . . .

DON'T MISS THESE
ALL-ACTION WESTERN SERIES
FROM THE BERKLEY PUBLISHING GROUP

THE GUNSMITH by J. R. Roberts
Clint Adams was a legend among lawmen, outlaws, and ladies. They called him . . . the Gunsmith.

LONGARM by Tabor Evans
The popular long-running series about U.S. Deputy Marshal Long—his life, his loves, his fight for justice.

LONE STAR by Wesley Ellis
The blazing adventures of Jessica Starbuck and the martial arts master, Ki. Over eight million copies in print.

SLOCUM by Jake Logan
Today's longest-running action Western. John Slocum rides a deadly trail of hot blood and cold steel.

THE GUNSMITH
148
AMBUSH MOON

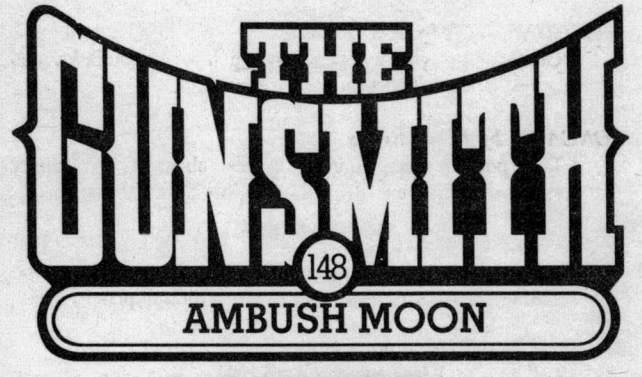

J. R. ROBERTS

JOVE BOOKS, NEW YORK

If you purchased this book without a cover, you should be aware that this book is stolen property. It was reported as "unsold and destroyed" to the publisher, and neither the author nor the publisher has received any payment for this "stripped book."

AMBUSH MOON

A Jove Book / published by arrangement with
the author

PRINTING HISTORY
Jove edition / April 1994

All rights reserved.
Copyright © 1994 by Robert J. Randisi.
This book may not be reproduced in whole
or in part, by mimeograph or any other means,
without permission. For information address:
The Berkley Publishing Group,
200 Madison Avenue,
New York, New York 10016.

ISBN: 0-515-11358-1

A JOVE BOOK®
Jove Books are published by The Berkley Publishing Group,
200 Madison Avenue,
New York, New York 10016.
JOVE and the "J" design are trademarks
belonging to Jove Publications, Inc.

PRINTED IN THE UNITED STATES OF AMERICA

10 9 8 7 6 5 4 3 2 1

ONE

The townspeople of Butte City, Colorado, were having a Fourth of July celebration on the day that the Gunsmith arrived at their high mountain town. Clint Adams had traveled all the way from the southwestern desert in search of the cool Rocky Mountains and the scent of pine. His tall black gelding, Duke, was lame, and the Gunsmith was footsore after having led the horse up through the northwest corner of the New Mexico Territory.

At the sight of the festive parade with its streaming red, white, and blue banners and the noisy, drunken fire companies with their oompah-pah bands each competing to be heard over the boisterous and celebrating crowd, the Gunsmith's weary face broke a smile.

He halted at the south edge of town and leaned against the gelding. Clint's eyes surveyed the community set nestled in a bowl surrounded by tall mountains. The Gunsmith noted the pretty ladies and the families of mostly mining men.

"I like the looks of this town," he said to his lame horse. "And we're both about played out and in bad need of some rest. What you say we hole up here for the summer and recuperate from the desert?"

Almost as if he understood, Duke dipped his head up and down. The Gunsmith's eyes followed the parade as it reached the end of town and then turned around and came marching back up the street.

"Looks like we'd best get out of the way," he said, leading his limping horse off on a side street.

Duke was not accustomed to so much noise and confusion. When the cymbals crashed, he snorted with anxiety.

"Easy," Clint said, stroking the animal's muzzle as the band passed. "They're just a bunch of folks having a good time. I'd even forgotten that this was Independence Day. And would you look at that covey of beauties!"

Clint removed his black, sweat-stained and dusty Stetson and waved it around in an overhead circle. One of the four lovely women aboard a wagon filled with straw noticed the ruggedly handsome stranger and blew him a kiss. The Gunsmith laughed, and the woman waved.

"Welcome to Butte City!"

"Thank you, ma'am! See you around!"

"Soon, I hope," the woman called. "I work at the Palace Saloon! Stop by and have a free drink on me—you look like you could use one!"

Clint blushed a little with embarrassment because he knew that he must look mighty rough-edged. His clothes were threadbare, and he was unwashed and unshaven. The sad truth of the matter was that he'd had a streak of bad luck with the cards over in Flagstaff, Arizona. And he still hadn't had any real chance to recoup his sagging fortunes by plying his trade, which was now gunsmithing. Maybe Butte City needed a gunsmith. Even if there was one already operating in this town, Clint thought the town might support another. His work was first-rate and his prices were as rock-bottom as his own current fortunes.

The parade reversed itself again at the south end of the street and came marching back. There was a lot of beer and whiskey flowing. The Gunsmith reached into his pockets. He had exactly two dollars left, and while he thirsted, Clint knew that he could not afford to spend his last couple dollars on whiskey. Duke was in need of a stall and the taste of oats as well as some doctoring. And Clint needed a bath, a shave, and a room while he tried to drum up some gunsmithing business.

Clint waited another half hour while the parade with its fire companies, wagonloads of citizens, and brass bands marched up and down the main street. Half the participants were drunk, and Clint saw one man upend a full bottle of beer into another's brass tuba causing the instrument to blow foam. When the marching finally ended, the crowds surged into the street, laughing and shouting. Several firecrackers were detonated. Women screamed, children scattered, and men roared with laughter. From what Clint could tell, Butte City was in the mood for celebrating, and there was going to be a lot more dancing and drinking before this day ended.

"Say, stranger," a whiskey-bottle-swigging miner called. "Ain't I seen you before?"

"You're probably seeing at least double," Clint replied with a tired grin. "Maybe three of me or more."

The miner closed one eye. He stopped, rocked precariously back and forth, and frowned. "Aw, I ain't that drunk . . . yet. Yeah, I seen you once before!"

"Great," Clint said. "How many liveries are in this town?"

The man blinked with confusion. "Liveries?"

"Yeah. Stables?"

"Just one," the miner said. "But it don't serve man nor beast whiskey!"

"Which direction?"

"To the livery?"

"Yes." Clint motioned to his horse. "He's lame, underweight, and played out. He needs a stall and rest."

"You don't look none too good yourself, if you don't mind my saying so."

"First comes my horse, then I take care of myself. Now where is the livery and is it well run?"

"Livery is at the other end of town. I'm a miner! How should I know if it's well run or not? The owner is named . . . aw, hell, I forgot. Quiet but friendly man and his father. But he don't drink, so I don't trust him."

Clint shook his head. "Well, that's a hell of a reason not to trust someone."

"It's a good reason! You drink, don't you?" the miner asked, narrowing his eyes suspiciously.

"Yeah, I've been known to wet my whistle."

"Here," the miner said, looking relieved as he shoved his bottle at the Gunsmith. "Drink up! Today is America's birthday!"

Clint took the bottle and held it up to the light. Not seeing any worms or foreign bodies floating around in the whiskey, he threw back his head and took a long pull. The whiskey burned a fiery swath down his gullet. It cut through the dust like a flash flood and struck the bottom of his belly to radiate heat like a blacksmith's forge.

"Ahh!" Clint said, smacking his lips. "Thanks. I needed that."

"Take another good pull," the miner said. "You looking for mine work?"

Clint took three full swallows. Tears sprang to his eyes because the whiskey had been flavored with Tabasco sauce. It tasted like chili and bit like a barnyard dog. Wiping his lips with the back of his arm, Clint said, "I'm no miner. I'm a gunsmith."

At this news, the miner's eyes widened with recognition. "Why, you're not just a gunsmith, you are the Gunsmith!"

Clint shrugged. "I've been called that by some but..."

"Some, hell! I saw you brace four men on the Comstock Lode two years ago and gun down two before the others turned their backs and ran for their lives. And they was all four damned fast and plenty quick on the shoot."

"They were the Wooten brothers," Clint said, remembering the gunfight. "Do you know whatever happened to the two that ran?"

"We hanged 'em! Caught up with 'em both down in Carson City and hanged 'em by a telegraph pole."

"Well," Clint said, "they deserved to hang."

"We could use a new sheriff right here in Butte City," the man said. "Hell, the law we got is corrupt."

"Not interested."

"Don't need another gunsmith, though. Maybe you'd better let me help you find a job in the mines. Pay is good. Two dollars a day. Enough to get drunk and whore it up on Saturday night."

"No thanks," Clint said, leading his horse out into the street. "But thanks for the whiskey."

"Hot damn!" the miner chortled, taking a long pull. "Just wait until I tell everyone that the Gunsmith has come to Butte City! Probably be a gunfight before you know it."

Clint heard that and said nothing as he continued up the crowded street. He did not advertise his past, but neither did he attempt to hide it. Sometimes younger men looking for a reputation came to gun him down, sometimes he was able to talk them out of getting shot. A man's past was like his face: you could hide it with a beard, but sooner or later it came back to haunt you in the mirror. Today, however, no one else seemed to recognize Clint, which was not especially surprising given his sorry appearance.

When the Gunsmith finally reached the livery, no one was around except an old man who had somehow managed to doze off despite the noisy celebrations.

He was an ancient fellow, ninety at least, with a darkly tanned and deeply wrinkled face, thin gray hair, and a corncob pipe resting in his bony old fists. Sitting propped up in a chair and wearing a gun belt and an outdated percussion pistol that seemed much too big and heavy for him, the old gent was snoring so peacefully that Clint did not have the heart to awaken him.

He led Duke into the barn and hunted up a stall while the gelding stood looking hopefully at a stack of hay.

"Right this way," Clint said, leading his horse over to a clean stall.

He unsaddled the horse, led him into the stall, and then closed the gate. Snatching up a pitchfork, Clint attacked the pile of hay, forking great wads of it into his horse's feed manger. Famished, Duke attacked the hay with a voracious appetite.

"That ought to keep you busy for the rest of the day," Clint said, resting the pitchfork up against the stall.

"Hello there?"

Clint turned to see a handsome, middle-aged man standing in the barn's doorway. He said, "Howdy. You got a new boarder."

"That's good. As long as it's a *paying* boarder."

"It is," Clint replied. "Though I admit that I'm a little short of funds right now."

"That's bad," the livery owner said. "Because I require to be paid in advance. You see, I've had a lot of folks run up a bill and then run out on me."

Clint sighed. "I'm an ex-sheriff," he explained. "And now I make my living gunsmithing and whatever else pays. What're the chances of gunsmithing in Butte City?"

"Not bad. We have one fella who thinks he can repair firearms—but he can't. He's no good. If you *are* good, I think you could do just fine. But I won't stake you a feed bill over it. By the way, my name is Bud York."

Clint shook hands and then pulled money out of his Levi's. "Here's two dollars. It's all the money I have, but I'll soon have more."

The man nodded but ignored the rumpled bills. He walked over to Duke's stall and leaned in to study the horse in the dim light. "That is one fine-looking animal, but you have to feed him once in a while."

"We've traveled a long hard trail. He's also lamed up in the right forefoot. He'll be needing some doctoring and shoeing."

"I do both, but it's on a cash—not credit—basis."

"Sure," Clint said. "Do you need any gunsmithing work that you'd take on trade?"

The liveryman studied the Gunsmith closely. "Might be that we can work something out. As a matter of fact, I'm sure of it. There's trouble—big trouble—brewing over at Aspen Gulch. People all over this county are up in arms, although you'd never know it the way they're drinking today."

"Why?"

"People getting ambushed over in Aspen Gulch and all around these parts."

"Outlaws?"

"Nope." Bud York frowned. "Most folks are starting to believe the Ute Indians are behind the bushwhackings."

"Now why would they think that?"

"Well, you see, the ambushers always kill during the time of the full moon."

Clint was puzzled. "You mean the only time that the ambushers strike is in full moonlight?"

"No, it just has to be the *time* of the full moon. Some of the ambushings have been at night but some in the day. No one saw the pattern until a few weeks ago. You see, these ambushings don't happen but four or five times a year."

"That's still enough to put the spook on a lot of folks," Clint said.

"It sure is. Now, there's a full moon tomorrow night, and you won't hardly see anyone outdoors after dark. And even during the day this place is an armed camp. It's ten times worse over in Aspen Gulch."

"What has all this got to do with Indians?"

"It is commonly thought that all the killing has something to do with a Ute Indian spiritual ceremony."

Clint snorted with derision. "I never heard of such a thing."

"Me neither," the liveryman admitted. "But then, I don't know doodly-squat about Indians."

"I do," Clint said. "And they're just as different as us white folks. There's good and bad, fighters and sleepers."

"Well," Bud said, "I'd *like* to be a sleeper like my father out there in that chair, but I've got no time for it."

Clint extended his money again.

"Naw, you keep it. You probably didn't notice, but my father is wearing an ancient Navy Colt. He once used it to kill an outlaw that tried to steal his horses. That pistol hasn't been in working condition for years. But it has a sentimental value and if you could . . ."

"Consider it done," Clint said. "Is there any place in town where I can get a room and a cheap but good meal?"

"Sure, but why don't you bed down in the stall next to your horse? It's clean and the weather is nice. No one will bother you and you can save that other dollar for eats."

"I might just do that," Clint said. "In fact, I'll just toss my saddle, bags, and bedroll in there."

"That'd be fine," Bud said. "I recommend the Glory Hole Café just up the street."

"Thanks."

Clint looked at his horse, then back at the liveryman. "This big gelding has saved my bacon more times than I can count. I'm damned worried about his lameness.

"Look," Clint said, picking up Duke's foot. "His shoes are paper-thin, causing his frog to touch the trail."

"That'll cause a rock bruise every time," Bud said. "No doubt about it, your horse is long overdue for a new set of shoes."

"I know. We've traveled some rocky trails since leaving the desert," Clint said, knowing that he should have had the animal freshly shod in Santa Fe. "Well, I'll look forward to hearing your opinion as to the cause of Duke's lameness after you've had a chance to look him over."

"I'll do that right now. Go get yourself something to eat. You look like a winter-starved lobo wolf."

"I appreciate your help," Clint said. "And I'll make it up . . ."

"I know that," Bud interrupted. "Just go along and get some food in your belly. By the time you return, I'll have a pretty good idea about your horse. Sometimes a new set of shoes will do wonders."

Clint nodded and headed back outside. Bud York was a hell of a fine man, the kind that judged a man by more than just his current physical appearance. Well, Clint thought, when I make a few dollars, Bud York will be the first in Butte City to get his share.

As he made his way through the crowd of celebrants, Clint saw an Indian standing in the shadows. The man was wrapped in a thin blanket and cowered under Clint's gaze. The Gunsmith smiled, but the Indian's fearful and wary expression did not change. Seeing the pathetic figure reminded Clint of the ambushings that had been taking place in this part of the country. He rejected outright the growing sentiment that they must have something to do with a Ute spiritual ceremony because they always took place during the time of the full moon.

As an ex-lawman with many years' experience, and also as a man who had traveled extensively throughout the West with more than his share of dealings with Indians, Clint thought the Utes unlikely of being ambushers. And although he did not know a great deal about the Ute people, he had always heard that they were forthright and upstanding. Ambushing lone white men during the time of the full moon just didn't make sense.

Then who was responsible and why? Clint involuntarily shrugged his shoulders. If he were still a lawman, it would be an interesting riddle, although it was his guess there was a very simple explanation to the string of deadly ambushes.

Murder, in the Gunsmith's professional opinion, was almost always an act of passion, and passion was rarely reasoned or complex.

TWO

Clint found the Glory Hole Café easy enough, and although the streets were packed with a happy crowd, the café was almost empty except for a blond waitress who bore telltale signs of hard living on her otherwise pretty face.

"What can I do for you, mister?" she asked, sizing up the Gunsmith's scruffy appearance.

"I'd like as much food as you can rustle up for fifty cents," Clint said, trying to hide his embarrassment.

"For fifty cents you can have all the fried potatoes you want, or about a pound of 'em and a couple of thick slabs of beef."

Clint took a seat. "And maybe a little gravy, bread, coffee, and some of that apple pie that you got under that counter glass?"

"You *are* a hungry dog."

"I plead guilty to the charge," Clint said, glancing at the apple pie.

The waitress brushed back a damp tendril of hair and studied him for a moment. "You look dead broke."

Clint fished out his two rumpled bills. "Right now, I'm a little short of funds. But that will soon change."

The woman was tall and full-bodied. Her china-blue eyes were framed by dark circles. Ten years earlier she had undoubtedly been a real beauty. Clint had seen too many of her kind who had been long overworked and left to fend for themselves on the frontier.

"I'll fix you up one hell of a good feed," she said. "Hell, why not? The boss is out getting drunk as a lord while I'm tending business. My name is Thelma."

"Clint Adams. That's quite a celebration out there."

"It sure is."

Thelma went into the kitchen, saying, "I can see that you're more interested in that apple pie than my conversation, so go ahead and help yourself."

"Thank you, ma'am!"

Thelma whipped a pint flask out of her dress, which she uncorked and sampled. "Clint, I bet you'd agree that it's high time us poor and downtrodden had a little fun in life too!"

"I agree," Clint said, scooping up the dripping pie and devouring it without concern for good table manners.

Thelma came out and watched until he had eaten the entire pie. She handed him a white linen napkin, saying, "Mister, you beat all. Where did you come from that there was no women to feed a handsome devil like yourself?"

"I've been all over. Most recently from Arizona and then New Mexico."

"That's desert country." Thelma poured him a cup of scalding black coffee. "Welcome to cool Colorado. And now that you've had dessert, I'll bring you a heaping plateful of beef and potatoes."

"Much obliged, Thelma. You and Bud York over at the livery are the only two people I've met so far in Butte City. You've both been real nice and uncommonly generous. Makes me think I'd like to summer here."

"You could do worse," Thelma called from the kitchen. "The mines are all hiring."

"I'm not a miner. I do gunsmithing."

"Too bad. We've got one of them already."

"Yeah," Clint called, "but from what I hear, he's not much good."

Clint wiped his face with a napkin and blew on his coffee to cool it down a little. He twisted around on his stool and saw that the marching up and down Main Street was finally over and the traditional patriotic speeches had begun. As a past sheriff of many towns, Clint had had his fill of both politicians and speeches. Even now, Clint could hear a stuffed shirt official addressing the crowd. The Gunsmith was relieved that he didn't have to suffer through that kind of thing anymore now that he was no longer a public servant.

"Here you go," Thelma said, setting on the countertop a plate of steaming potatoes swimming in gravy, fresh rolls, and a steak thick enough to be called a roast.

Clint wasted no time in attacking the feast. He had not eaten anything but his own trail cooking for a week and he was famished.

"My, my," Thelma said, folding her arms across her ample bosom. "I haven't seen a man eat like you in a long, long time. Things have been good in Butte City as long as I've been working here. The mines are paying off with both gold and silver. Money is plentiful and there's enough work."

"With your fine looks," Clint said, "I'll bet you do pretty good yourself."

"I do all right," Thelma admitted. "I still have my regular breakfast and dinner admirers, and I do flirt with my favorites. They're generous and fun to tease."

Clint sipped at his coffee, but it was still much too hot to drink.

"Yeah," Thelma said, her blue eyes a little wistful, "I still do all right. I work here in the day and do a little hostessing over at the Palace Saloon at night."

Clint knew what that generally meant.

"But I'm no whore!" Thelma said quickly, as if she could read his thoughts.

With a mouthful of potatoes, Clint grunted, "No, ma'am!"

Thelma relaxed. "I just . . . smooch up to the boys and get 'em ready for the *real* whores, you understand."

"That's about what I figured," Clint said. "I can see that you're a very respectable woman just trying to make an honest living."

Thelma smiled again. "Oh, I'd trade my respectability for a wealthy husband, and honesty ain't got a thing to do with how well a person manages to make a living."

"No, ma'am," Clint said, not about to disagree.

The Gunsmith had met plenty of women just like Thelma. They were good-hearted to a fault. When they latched onto a man, they were loyal and loving. Trouble was, they usually latched onto the wrong men and got their hearts broken again and again. Thelma was telling Clint between the lines that she wasn't expecting much, but she was looking for a good, honest man. One who would love and not leave her like the others.

"You married?" Thelma asked a little shyly.

"No."

"I've been married twice. First one got himself hanged for horse thieving. He wasn't worth much. I married again, but I didn't do any better because Art farted so often it was enough to make a goat gag. He couldn't keep an indoor job and he didn't want to work outdoors. I have to admit that Art was a sweet-talker, but he was worthless."

"Sounds like," Clint said, mopping gravy from his plate with a slice of buttered bread.

Thelma sighed. "Art loved me, but he loved other women too. He ran off with one and took her over to live in Santa Fe. You probably seen—or smelled— him if you were there anytime at all."

"I don't believe I did."

"Art was a big man. About three hundred pounds. I hear he took up being a mule skinner because he smelled up things so bad. But I bet he gassed them mules to death, same as he nearly gassed me."

"No more husbands for you, huh, Thelma?"

She leaned over the counter so that he could admire the upper slopes of her twin peaks. When he'd had a good look, Thelma straightened and said, "Well now, I didn't say that. If the right man came along, I'd consider marrying him. But I'm not counting on no prince dancin' into my life."

Clint's coffee had finally cooled enough to drink. He emptied the cup and said, "Thelma, that makes sense."

"There's a few good men in this country," she said, refilling his cup with the scalding brew, "but most are worthless."

"Uh-huh."

"What kind of a man are you, Clint?"

"I'm no prize," he admitted as he mopped his plate to a shine with the last bit of his bread.

"How'd such a handsome fella like yourself fall on such hard times?"

"I had an uncommon streak of bad luck at cards."

Thelma shook her head and sighed. "You're a gambler. That's one of the worst kinds. My first husband, the one that got hanged, he was a gambler too. I swear he was the worst poker player in Colorado, but he thought he was the best. He stole horses to sell for gambling money. The fool most always lost. He never understood that cards was the true cause of his ruination."

"I don't gamble *that* much," Clint said. "For years I was a lawman. Now, I mostly just gunsmith and sometimes I do very well at it."

"Then maybe you can make a go of it even if..."

Thelma's voice died, and the woman paled. The change in Thelma was so dramatic that the Gunsmith swiveled around on his stool. He saw two big, well-dressed men standing just outside the window of the café. They appeared to be about to enter but were now arguing.

Turning back to Thelma, Clint asked, "What's wrong?"

"It's the boss! Henry wasn't supposed to be back today! And he's got Luke with him! Oh, Jesus, I'm in a fix now!"

Clint didn't understand why the woman was so upset. "What's wrong? You've been working."

Thelma got real busy wiping the counter. "If the boss discovers that I let you eat a pie and a big meal for just fifty cents, I'll catch hell! He's got a terrible temper when he's been drinking."

"Here," Clint said, digging out a dollar. "This ought to be enough to keep him from getting upset."

But Thelma didn't seem to be listening. "Henry has been trying to corner me in the kitchen. Both of them are meaner than snakes when they've been drinking."

Clint started to ask the woman why she didn't quit if she was that pressured by them, but there wasn't time before the door banged open and the two large men barged inside.

"Thelma!"

Thelma disappeared into the kitchen. The Gunsmith could hear her banging pots like crazy.

"Luke, I'll be right back. Have some apple pie if you're of a mind. Just leave your money on the . . ."

"I finished it off," Clint said, forcing a smile at the bigger of the pair. "Damned tasty."

"You ate the whole goddamn pie?"

"That's right."

"Thelma! Goddammit, get out here!"

Clint came off his stool. He could see that both men were drunk and itching to humiliate and raise hell with poor Thelma. They were bullies. The kind that Clint had hated his entire life.

When the boss started to move around the counter toward the kitchen, the Gunsmith grabbed his arm. "My name is Clint. I'm a gunsmith, and if you need any expert work, I'll be around town for a while. I plan to eat here a lot. Good food and even better service."

Henry yanked his arm free. "You look like a damned misfit to me! Thelma, did you get this deadbeat's money before he ate?"

Thelma appeared from the kitchen and anyone could see that she was trembling. "I did."

"Hand it over."

"Pleasant man," Clint hissed out of the corner of his mouth to Luke. "I imagine you and Henry are a whole lot of fun when you drink together."

"Shut up!" Luke snarled. "I had my heart set on apple pie and you ate the whole son of a bitch! Goddamn starving hog."

Clint reached down and casually picked up his coffee. With a smile and a flick of his wrist, he tossed the steaming liquid into Luke's eyes.

AMBUSH MOON

"Ahhh!" the man screamed, slapping his meaty face.

Clint knew that Henry would be on him in about two seconds and that he had better drop Luke hard and fast. That being the case, he hooked the bigger man in the solar plexus, and when Luke's mouth flew open, Clint stuffed the man's howl with the knuckles of his right hand. Luke bounced off the counter, eyes glazed but a curse on his lips.

"Clint, look out!"

The Gunsmith whirled a split second before Henry would have walloped him from behind with a heavy, cast-iron frying pan. Clint's right fist caught Henry in the mouth, and the big man backpedaled. Luke grabbed him from behind, and the Gunsmith smashed his boot heel down Luke's shin, causing the man to release his hold. Clint whirled and lashed out with all his strength and, this time, Luke hit the waxed floor skidding.

But before Clint could pivot and defend himself, Henry's fist clubbed him like a mallet and Clint also hit the floor. He looked up to see Henry's boot coming at his face. The Gunsmith dropped flat, rolled, and struggled up to his feet as Henry charged.

Clint got tangled up in a table and it overturned on him. Before he could extricate himself, Henry had landed on his chest and was raining blows against Clint's head. The man's weight felt like a mountain, and it was all that Clint could do to try and deflect some of the blows with his upraised arms.

A gonging sound brought an end to the struggle even more quickly than it had begun. Clint looked up to see Thelma with the big cast-iron frying pan. Henry's eyes crossed and he made a garbled sound in his throat before Thelma reared back and with two hands on the handle bashed the big man square in the face.

Even Clint winced at the hollow metallic sound of iron striking skull. Henry went over backward and quivered as his nose flowed blood.

"Are you all right?" Thelma cried, dropping the pan and kneeling by the Gunsmith's side.

"Yeah," he said, the entire left side of his face numbing. "Did you kill him?"

"I hope so!" Thelma breathed, looking scared but determined.

Clint's ears were ringing and he felt woozy as he crawled over to Henry's side. The man was unconscious, but his pulse was strong and steady. He was, however, bleeding from his ears, and the Gunsmith knew that he had suffered a bad concussion.

"I think we had better get this man a doctor," Clint said, struggling to his feet.

"Is he going to die?"

"I don't think so, but if he doesn't, I have a hunch he's never going to be quite the same."

"I hope not!" Thelma cried. "He and Luke are animals!"

Clint nodded. "Let's find that doctor," he said, draping an arm across Thelma's shoulders. "And then I think you'd better start thinking about a new job."

THREE

That evening found the Gunsmith immersed in a hot, soapy bathtub with a glass of whiskey in his hand to further ease his aches and pains.

"You look much, much handsomer now that I've shaved you," Thelma said. "In fact, you'd really be quite a prize if you weren't so poor."

The Gunsmith laughed. "Thelma, if I didn't know you better, I'd think you had a purely mercenary heart."

Thelma was wearing a man's nightshirt and a smile. She leaned forward on her chair and touched the Gunsmith's bruised face. "I'm sorry that you had to take such punishment, but I'm sure glad that you were there to protect me."

"You're better off without that job," Clint said. "Henry and Luke were both mean. If I were sheriff of this town, I'd figure out a way to have them arrested."

"I'm going to have to leave this town," Thelma said. "If I don't, I'm afraid that Henry is going to find a way to get even. You're also in some danger."

23

Clint sipped his whiskey. The bath felt wonderful and he'd sipped enough whiskey so that he no longer felt the worst of his pains. "If either of them so much as gives me a cross look, I'll make them wish they'd left town."

"You don't understand," Thelma said. "Henry is in cahoots with the sheriff who is beholden to the mayor. Between the three of them, they can make things rough for us. I think we *both* ought to leave town—tonight."

"Uh-uh," Clint said. "In the first place, I'm too beat up and wrung out. In the second place, my horse is lame and in bad need of rest, and in the third place, I think we need to spend a little time getting better acquainted."

Thelma leaned over the edge of the big tub and kissed the Gunsmith full on the lips. He set his whiskey down and began to unbutton her shirt. "Let's take a look at what you got for me, honey."

Thelma had even more than expected. Her breasts were full, and when the Gunsmith drew them to his mouth, Thelma sighed with pleasure. She began to squirm as the Gunsmith's lips and tongue laved her dark nipples.

"I think you're right about us needing some time to get better acquainted," she panted, reaching into the water to find Clint's stiffening rod.

"Want a bath?"

"I can think of things I'd rather do," she purred, her hand working his manhood into a powerful erection.

"Come on in; the water feels good and so do you,"

Clint suggested, pushing Thelma's nightshirt aside and almost dragging her into the tub, which immediately overflowed.

"It's going to run through the floor and seep through the ceiling below," Thelma groaned as she spread her legs wide and sat down on the Gunsmith's throbbing rod.

"Yeah," he said, not giving a damn. "Whoever lives under us will think it's starting to rain."

"Mrs. Watson lives down below and she's a fury. She'll raise cain."

"Let her," Clint gritted, gripping Thelma's buttocks and driving his rod in and out of the woman.

For the next ten minutes, Clint and Thelma splashed and gasped and giggled, playing with each other until their bodies tingled with the need for release.

"I don't know how much longer we can keep this up," Thelma breathed. "I'm starting to . . ."

"Hey up there! Thelma! What the hell is going on?"

"Nothing!" Thelma gasped. "Nothing at all, Mrs. Watson!"

"Well, it sure as hell isn't raining outside. You got a man pissing on the floor, or what?"

"No, ma'am!" Thelma cried as Clint's hard body slammed up and down harder and harder, causing even more water to spill over the edge of the tub.

"Thelma! What the hell is going on?"

"Nothing, Mrs. . . . . oh! Oh! OH!"

"Thelma?"

Thelma began to bounce up and down. She threw

her head back and moaned with pleasure.

"Thelma! Are you all right?"

"Y . . . yes!"

Clint drew Thelma down, and his hips pistoned his seed into her until she slumped over on him with her bottom twitching.

"Thelma! Thelma, I'm coming up there right now!"

"No!"

"Let her," Clint said. "Maybe it will give the old bat something to dream about."

But Thelma would hear none of that. She leapt out of the tub and grabbed up her nightshirt. But she slipped on the wet floor and landed hard on her behind. Before she could recover, Mrs. Watson was pounding on the door.

"I know you got a man in there, Thelma. And he's pissing on your floor! You make him stop that, you understand me?"

"Yes, Mrs. Watson," Thelma wheezed, trying to keep from breaking into gales of laughter. "He's got to stop sometime, Mrs. Watson."

"Well, he must be a horse's ass to act that way. Thelma, you need to find a better class of man!"

"I'll try, Mrs. Watson."

"See that you do," the old lady shouted. "I never seen the likes of such behavior. It's gonna smell something terrible the next time we get a hot Chinook through this country!"

Clint slid beneath the water and howled bubbles. Gasping for breath, he resurfaced and looked sheepishly at Thelma, who was sitting on the floor with her hands covering her face and tears of laughter running down her cheeks.

"Jesus, aren't we a pair?" Thelma finally managed to say.

"We are for a fact," the Gunsmith replied.

The next time they made love, it was in bed. It was not as messy and almost as good as the bathtub. The Gunsmith rode Thelma until she squealed and bucked like a filly. When he erupted into her the second time, he felt fire spread through his loins and he knew that he was spent.

"Are you hungry again?" she whispered as the last rays of sun filtered through their upstairs hotel window.

"I am," he admitted. "And I should go over to the livery and check on my horse."

"You put a lot of stock in him, don't you?"

"Yes," Clint replied. "We've been together for several years now and he's like a big friend. I feel badly about letting him get so run-down."

Thelma climbed out of bed. "Let's get dressed and we'll both go see your horse. Afterward, we'll find a place for supper."

"But not the Glory Hole Café."

"No," Thelma said. "Definitely not."

There was fire in the sky as the sun glowed a deep orange along the western horizon. Atop the highest peaks, snow glistened like a field of diamonds, and as Clint walked along beside Thelma, he thought that he had never seen a more spectacular sunset. Turning to Thelma, he saw how the sunset bathed her features and her thick mane of blond hair in a golden light.

"You're a fine specimen of womanhood," he said, noting the admiring glances that Thelma received as they made their way toward the livery.

Thelma blushed. "They say that a woman who has just been made love to has a glow to her skin. But in this case, I think it is just the sunset."

"I don't know about that."

"I do." Thelma squeezed his arm. "I was the prettiest girl in Denver when I was growing up. I really was. But I'm not a girl any longer. You can see the crow's-feet at the corners of my eyes and . . ."

"Shhh!" Clint stopped, took her into his arms, and kissed her, not caring who watched. When he drew back, he said, "I think you're still a handsome woman and a tiger in bed."

"You shhh!" Thelma said, blushing again.

When they arrived at the livery, Bud York came out of his combination office and sleeping quarters to greet them. When he saw Thelma, he smiled broadly. "Miss Boren! You look prettier than a hundred-dollar bill."

"Why, thank you, Bud!"

"How's Duke?" Clint asked, moving past the man to reach his horse.

"I got good news," the liveryman said. "Your horse just has a bad rock bruise like we were hoping."

Clint expelled a sigh of relief. "That is good news. How long will he be laid up?"

"We should give him at least two weeks. I really can't shoe the animal until there is some healing."

"Two weeks is fine," the Gunsmith said. "We both need the rest and fattening."

"I heard about the fight at the Glory Hole Café," Bud said, his smile fading. "I guess Henry is in pretty rough shape. Luke is saying that Thelma brained him with a big frying pan."

"I did," Thelma said. "And I'd do it all over again."

Bud nodded, his face somber. "Luke has been telling folks that he's going to get even with the both of you."

"Is that right?" Clint said. "Well, anytime he wants he can come looking for me and we'll settle the issue in a hurry."

"I doubt he'll do that," Bud said. "You see, by now, everyone in Butte City knows who you really are."

Thelma frowned. "What is that supposed to mean?"

Bud turned to Thelma. "Don't you know that this is Clint Adams? One of the most celebrated gunfighters and ex-sheriffs in the entire West?"

"You never said anything about being famous!"

"Didn't see much point." The Gunsmith winked. "Besides, it wouldn't have gotten me anything extra, would it?"

Thelma's cheeks colored. "You're awful. Just awful!"

Bud York shifted dirt back and forth with the toe of his boot. "I can see that you two have already gotten very well acquainted. Might as well tell you something else that might prove very useful."

"What's that?" Clint asked, hearing the warning tone in the man's voice.

"Well, there's some speculation that the sheriff is

going to arrest Miss Boren for assault with intent to kill."

"What?" Thelma cried.

"You damned near knocked Henry's brains out," the liveryman said. "The doctor isn't even sure the man will ever quite be the same."

"Good!" Thelma exclaimed, stomping down her foot. "I hope I have forever changed his thinking. He was a despicable person and a bully. Why, you know what a terrible reputation he had when he got drunk. He'd beat up people half his size and then stomp them."

"I know," Bud said. "I know. Henry and I went at it about a year ago. Toughest man I ever whipped."

"You whipped Henry?"

"I did," Bud said. "But I had the spoke of a wagon wheel in my hand while he was slicing at me with his bowie knife. I just happened to get in the first good lick. Dropped him cold."

"Good for you," Clint said. "And thanks for the warning about Luke."

"Watch your backs," Bud advised. "Luke isn't as tough as Henry, but he's sneakier. And he's priming himself with whiskey."

"A drunk never hits what he aims for," the Gunsmith said. "The trouble is, they often spray their bullets around and drill some innocent bystander."

"The sheriff ought to put him in jail until he sobers up," Bud said. "But our sheriff isn't much."

"We'll be watching for Luke," Clint said.

"I guess that you'd just as soon I stowed your bedroll in my office for the time being, huh?" Bud asked, eyes moving back and forth between Clint and Thelma.

"Yeah," Clint said. "I think I've found more . . . comfortable accommodations. But I sure appreciate your offer, and I might as well get my saddlebags. I'll return to see Duke in the morning."

"You won't see much change for a few days."

"I can already see that he's perkier."

Clint collected his saddlebags and bid the liveryman good night. "Nice fella," he said when they were out of earshot. "Thelma, how come you never hooked up with Bud York?"

She looked strangely at him. "Bud never showed any interest in me."

"I could tell that he's real interested the way that he was staring at you."

"Must be that lovemaking glow," Thelma said happily.

They found another café, and the Gunsmith made sure that they got a table in the back of the room where he'd have plenty of time to see trouble coming. Thelma paid for their supper and when they were through, they headed back to her hotel. The streets were empty now, but the saloons continued to do a huge holiday business. There were a few drunks asleep on the sidewalk, but most folks seemed to be either too whiskey-soaked to cause trouble, or too happy. Thelma was greeted by most everyone with genuine affection and respect.

"There will be some big heads in the morning besides Henry's," Thelma predicted. "I know most of these fellas, and they'll be hurting."

"They're used to it," Clint said. "Miners are among the toughest men I've ever met."

"Tougher than ex-sheriffs?"

"At least as tough." Clint thumbed back his hat and drank in the scent of pines as they neared the hotel. "I sure am glad to hear that my horse is going to be all right."

"Me too. Clint, I . . ."

A muzzle flash stabbed out of the darkness between two buildings they'd just passed. Clint's arm instinctively tightened around Thelma and he drove her to the sidewalk, his right hand scooting for his six-gun. He heard a second shot strike the woman just as his gun came up and he fired into the shadows between buildings. He fired again and again; muzzle flashes matched those probing at him from the darkness.

The Gunsmith heard a grunt of pain and then the sound of boots hammering into the night. As much as Clint wanted to go after the assassin, he knew that his first obligation was to do everything humanly possible to save poor Thelma.

"Thelma!" he whispered urgently, rolling the woman onto her back. She was conscious, but bleeding heavily from a wound in her side and another in the shoulder.

"Someone get Dr. Potter!" the Gunsmith shouted as men poured out of the saloons. "We need a doctor!"

Dr. Potter, whom Clint had taken Henry to earlier, arrived a few minutes later. He took one look at Thelma and said, "Let's get her to my office. Quick!"

Clint had more than enough help. Half running, half stumbling, they rushed Thelma down the street to the doctor's office and laid her on an examination table.

"Everyone out!" the doctor, a white-haired, scholarly looking gentleman ordered, grabbing a lantern and turning up the wick so that he could take a good look at the wounds. "Everyone!"

"Not me," Clint said. "She took the bullets I should have taken. I'm not going anywhere."

"Can you stomach surgery? Maybe even assist?"

"Hell yes!"

The doctor bent over the side wound pumping dark blood. "If that bullet hit an organ, Thelma is as good as dead."

"How can you tell?"

"I can't until I go in after it," the doctor said. "Without surgery, she hasn't a prayer."

"Tell me what to do," Clint said. "I've had plenty of experience at this sort of thing."

"I'm glad to hear that," the physician said as he collected his surgical instruments, "but right now, I'd rather you were a man of God because He might just be the only power that can save her."

That was not what the Gunsmith wanted to hear.

"Wash your hands in this solution of alcohol," the doctor ordered, splashing the solution over his own hands. "Who shot her?"

"Fella that I whipped earlier named Luke."

"Are you sure?"

"I will be when I find him," the Gunsmith vowed. "In fact, if he isn't already dead, there's no doubt that he's in desperate need of your services."

The doctor looked up at the Gunsmith and started to say something to him, but just then Thelma cried out in pain and began to thrash. After that, it was all that both men could do to prepare her for the scalpel.

FOUR

The Gunsmith had seen too many doctors put the knife to gunshot victims. At least a half dozen times Clint himself had also undergone surgery to remove a bullet. Far more often, he had been forced to cut his own bullet from an outlaw in an attempt to save the man's life and return him to jail, prison, or even the hangman's gallows.

But Thelma's surgery was far more complex than anything Clint could have hoped to perform. The first assassin's bullet to strike Thelma was not life-threatening. Once the doctor had stemmed the bleeding, he observed that the bullet that had struck Thelma in the shoulder had passed completely through her body. Even Clint could have cleaned and packed it to the satisfaction of a real doctor. But the second bullet still lodged in Thelma's side was another matter because it was definitely a killer.

"All right," the doctor said, soaking a wad of cotton in chloroform, which filled the room with its sickeningly sweet odor. "Your job is to use these forceps and help me to tie off the bleeders. You'll also need to pinch down tight if I happen to accidentally cut through a big blood vessel."

The Gunsmith nodded. The blood was welling from the side wound, and Thelma's face no longer had a rosy glow but was the color of a pale candle.

"What are her chances, Doc?"

"I don't know," Potter admitted. "Thelma is still young and quite strong. She might survive."

That was not the reassuring news that Clint longed to hear. He clamped his jaw, and the doctor gently placed the chloroformed cotton ball over Thelma's nose. The powerful drug acted quickly. Thelma's breathing became slow and easy. The doctor continued to hold the anesthetic to her face, constantly raising her eyelids to observe Thelma's pupils. A moment later, he would carefully check her pulse.

"I think she's deep enough now to start," Potter said. "If I give her too much chloroform, her heart, already overtaxed from the loss of blood, will stop."

Dr. Potter chose a scalpel. Bending over Thelma and using the back of the scalpel, he drew an imaginary incision.

"All right," he said to himself, "we can't wait for divine inspiration." With a swift, sure stroke he made a deep incision right through the bullet wound.

"How come so little bleeding?"

"It's the anesthetic. By greatly slowing the heart and respiration, it retards the bleeding. The danger is in not maintaining enough blood flow to the brain."

Even as he spoke, Potter was using his forceps to clamp off bleeders and directing Clint to do the same to the ones that he pointed out.

After a few minutes, Potter said, "Let's tie a few of these off, Mr. Adams, before we run out of forceps when we might most need them."

Clint was sweating profusely. He was worried that the doctor would ask him to help tie off the bleeders, but his fears proved groundless. When they had the bleeding satisfactorily under control, Potter made the incision deeper yet. There were more vessels to tie off. Finally, the surgeon selected a large forceps, eased it into the wound, and closed his eyes.

"Why are you closing your eyes?"

"You can do this better by feel and that sensory perception is enhanced."

It made sense to the Gunsmith.

"There," Potter said, after what seemed an eternity. "I think I've reached the bullet. It feels different than any natural mass in the body, such as bone. It is metal against metal and . . . yes, I have it!"

An instant later, Potter was holding up the misshapen lead slug. "Forty-five caliber, wouldn't you say?"

"Definitely." Clint wiped his brow with the back of his bare and bloodied arm.

"Let's tie off these last vessels one by one as we remove the forceps. I'll pack the wound with disinfectant and hope that she survives."

"Do you know Thelma?"

"Quite well," the doctor said. "Everyone knows and loves Thelma. I'll bet that she gets at least one marriage proposal a week. Turns them all down."

"But why? She was killing herself working at the Glory Hole Café and she sure wasn't getting rich, even with generous tips from her customers."

"Who knows the heart and mind of a woman?" the doctor said as he worked swiftly. "Thelma has endured a lot of grief in her life, almost all of it from men. I think that she's afraid to get married again."

"I see."

"She should marry Bud York," the doctor said. "He's the best prospect in Butte City, but he's painfully shy with women and he doesn't cut a fancy figure."

"Bud is a fine man," Clint agreed. "He'd make a good husband and father."

The doctor worked in silence for the next forty minutes. He tied off the bleeders, packed both bullet wounds, and spent a long time with his bandaging. It was easy to see that Dr. Potter was a perfectionist.

"How was Henry's head when you examined him earlier?" Clint finally asked.

The doctor grinned. "Henry has a severe concussion, but there is no sign of permanent brain damage—at least any that wasn't already there from his heavy and chronic drinking."

The doctor looked up at Clint. "My assessment is that Henry will live to beat the shit out of more weaker and smaller men. I shouldn't say this—it violates the spirit of my own Hippocratic oath—but the world would be better off with fewer of his kind."

AMBUSH MOON

"Sometimes," Clint observed, "a serious injury like that will put fear into a bully. Make him as meek as a lamb."

"I hope it does," Potter said, "but that would put a considerable dent in my medical practice."

Clint looked up to see that Potter had the slightest hint of a grin on his lips. "Doc, it seems to me that if you can joke at a time like this, it must mean that you think Thelma is going to live."

"I think she will," Potter announced, stepping back to admire his handiwork. "In a day or two, if all goes well and the wounds appear to be healing cleanly, she can be moved back to her hotel room."

"I'll see that Thelma has the best of care."

"By you?"

"Why . . . I hadn't thought much about it. But yes, if necessary. This woman took a pair of bullets meant for me."

"And as soon as you can leave, you're going to find Luke and gun him down, is that right?"

"Maybe." Clint frowned. "If you've got something to say, spit it out plain."

"You've a reputation for being a fast gun. Also, it's said that you were a credit to the law. I suggest you apply the law and bring Luke in alive. Let a jury decide if he was the one that shot Thelma."

"Oh, he shot her all right."

"You actually saw him?"

"No, but . . ."

"Maybe it was someone else."

"What are you driving at?"

"There's been a string of assassinations and ambushes. Tonight there is a full moon."

"Doc, are you actually suggesting that some Indian was hiding in the shadows and shot Thelma as we passed? That this was just a random shooting?"

"I'm not suggesting anything of the sort. But I sincerely do hope that you'll feel obligated to find out exactly who that person—or persons—might be."

"It was Luke," Clint said with plenty of conviction. "And I'll take him alive, if possible, but dead if necessary."

Since there was nothing left that the Gunsmith could do to help Thelma, he washed his hands, retrieved his Stetson, and turned to say good-bye to Thelma.

"I'll stay with her the rest of the night," the doctor promised. "If everything looks good in the morning and her color improves, I think we'll be out of the woods."

Clint was about to say something about how grateful he was to Potter and how fortunate the people of Butte City were to have such a fine doctor and surgeon, but he was interrupted by a loud pounding on the door.

"Who is it?" the doctor shouted.

"It's Herb Casey, Doc. There's been another ambush! You got to come quick!"

Dr. Potter reached for his coat and medicinal kit, but Clint blocked his path. "Wait a minute! You can't leave Thelma alone!"

"That's right," Potter said. "You're going to have to stay with her instead of me."

"But I'm no doctor! I couldn't do anything if she..."

"You could say a few prayers and not let her die alone," Potter said. "And at this point, I doubt that I could do much of anything more."

Clint stepped aside. Luke would have to wait for a few more hours. That the man was wounded, Clint had no doubt. The question was, how badly was he wounded? Clint had only seen the muzzle flash of the drunken ambusher's Colt when he'd returned fire. It was possible that Luke had just been winged and was even now riding hard to save his life.

"I'll be back as soon as I can," Dr. Potter said. "Just stay close to Thelma. She'll be coming out from under that anesthesia within an hour or two. It's a dangerous time."

"You'd better be back by then!"

Potter looked at him but said nothing before he disappeared out the door into the moonlight.

The next few hours passed very slowly. There was little that the Gunsmith could do except hover close to Thelma and try to keep her warm and comfortable. Finally, the doctor returned.

"What happened?"

"It was a job for the mortician," Potter said, going to his cabinet and finding a bottle of liquor. "The man was a friend of mine. His name was Abe Long. He was a good and decent man, and someone cut him down as he was sitting on his porch beside his wife."

Clint watched the doctor toss down a series of gulps of whiskey, then cork the bottle and return it to its resting place. "How is she?"

"She seems to be resting comfortably." Clint's hand dropped to his six-gun. "I've got to go find Luke now."

"Yeah," Potter said, looking upset and distracted. "And after you've shot him, see if you can find out who is killing folks in these parts. That's the real trouble we all are facing."

Clint nodded. The doctor was clearly distraught and would be better left alone. At the door, Clint said, "You did one hell of a job with Thelma."

"Thanks."

"And maybe I can't repay you with money, but I can get to the bottom of these killings."

The doctor looked at him with haunted eyes. "Then by all means, please, do so!"

Clint dipped his chin and headed out the door.

FIVE

Clint headed for the nearest watering hole to get information on where he might find Luke. When he entered the raucous Palace Saloon, he walked right up to the bar, drew his gun, and banged its butt on the bar top.

"Listen up!" he shouted, loud enough to silence the din. "I'm sure that you have all heard about Thelma being ambushed. I'm happy to announce that she will live."

The entire saloon erupted in cheers. When they finally subsided, Clint said, "What I need to do is find the man that tried to ambush me and shot Thelma instead. I think that man was Luke."

"Luke who?" a mule skinner asked.

"Luke Bradley," a man leaning on the bar said. "The same fella whose ass the Gunsmith whipped along with Henry Reed in the Glory Hole Café earlier. You heard about that!"

The mule skinner was drunk on his feet. Feeling the eyes of everyone on him, he giggled nervously. "Oh yeah! I did hear about that fight. Musta been a good one."

"What makes you think that Luke was the son of a bitch that shot Thelma?" a big, whiskey-soaked miner wearing red suspenders and a derby hat cocked jauntily over one eye demanded. "Most of us think that it was one of them sneaky damned Ute Indians who shot her in the dark."

Clint took a step back to escape the miner's foul breath. "I don't know much about the Ute Indians," he admitted, "but it doesn't make a damned bit of sense to me that they'd be the ones behind the so-called full moon ambushes."

The miner stepped in close to the Gunsmith, balling his fists. "The hell you say!"

Clint decided to avoid, if at all possible, a fight. He'd much prefer to handle this with diplomacy and logic. But it was not going to be very easy.

"Listen," he said to everyone, "why would the Ute people set themselves up to be the victims of retribution?"

"Of what?" the big miner asked, trying to understand the Gunsmith's question.

"Why would the Utes be stupid enough to anger the whites and risk being wiped out?" Clint asked. "And what kind of an Indian ceremony would call for ambushing and killing people only during the time of the full moon?"

The miner was clearly befuddled. Feeling the others waiting for him to reply, he blustered and struggled for an answer. Having none, he finally stammered, "Why . . . why Indians have always done strange damned things!"

"That's ridiculous," Clint argued. "I've never heard

of an Indian people that shot women from ambush to gain face or respect."

The miner wiped his running nose with the back of his hand. He looked to his companions for help and when he found none, he turned back to Clint. "Mister, you sound like a goddamn Injun lover to me!"

The Gunsmith could see that the miner was working himself up to throw what he hoped would be a knockout punch. The man was big and he was belligerent. Clint did not want to fight again because his hands were still very sore and puffy from the beating they'd administered to Luke and Henry.

"Listen," he said, trying to be reasonable, "I'm *not* an Indian lover. What I am is an ex-lawman who learned by hard experience to weigh the facts. Weigh and study them and base your conclusions on them."

Clint paused to make sure that everyone was listening and, when he spoke, it was plenty loud enough for everyone present to hear. "The facts are that Luke made a threat against my life. He was also drunk and wild for revenge. That definitely makes him my number one suspect for ambushing Thelma."

Clint could feel the rough crowd shifting to his more reasonable point of view. "I'll be the first to admit that I've just arrived in Butte City. Some of you have probably heard that I have a reputation for this kind of trouble. But what I really came here to do was make a few honest dollars gunsmithing and escape the desert heat. All that changed when

Luke gunned down Thelma. So now, I need your help in finding the man."

"Luke is a friend of mine," the big miner said, sensing that the tide was running strong in Clint's favor. "He's bought me a drink or two."

"That doesn't count for anything," Clint snapped with impatience.

"It does to me!"

Clint saw the miner plant his feet on the sawdust floor, saw him dip his right shoulder and cock back his fist an instant before he would unleash a powerful uppercut.

The Gunsmith's already bruised right hand flashed to the Colt at his side. The six-gun came up in one swift, clean movement. It struck the miner against the side of his head. The miner cried out in pain and dropped to one knee.

"You bastard!" he sobbed, shaking his head and hanging onto the bar for support.

"I'll do it a second time and I guarantee that it won't leave you standing. Now get the hell out of here and go sober up before you really get hurt."

The miner drew his hand away from his temple and his fingers were covered with blood. He stared at the blood and paled. With a strangled cry, he climbed back on his feet and staggered toward the door.

Clint holstered his gun. "I didn't want to do that, but I guess everyone here can see I had no choice. I still need to find Luke Bradley and that means that I need some help."

"If you find the man, are you planning to kill him?"

AMBUSH MOON

a handsome young gambler dressed in a black frock coat, starched white shirt, and black tie asked, pushing through the crowd to address the Gunsmith.

"Not if I can help it," Clint replied. "But the man may already be dying. I managed to get off a couple of shots after he dropped Thelma. Thelma's ambusher is wounded, I can say that with certainty, and he may even be dead."

The gambler looked at the rough workingmen who provided his fancy style of living. "Luke isn't a miner."

"What does he do?"

"He has a room in town, but he spends most of his time at a ranch called the Rocking Horse, which is located about five miles north of town. The men Luke keeps company with haven't any cattle or horses. The ranch isn't even fenced, so I don't know what they do out there."

"And nobody has even bothered to ask?"

"Nope. Might not be the healthiest thing to do," the gambler said.

Clint understood what the man was saying. "Thanks for the information and directions. When I get there, you can be sure that I'll remember to ask."

The Gunsmith started to turn and head for the door, but a hard voice stopped him in his tracks. "Get your hands up. I'm Sheriff Denton, and you're under arrest."

Clint raised his hands and turned around to face a tall, cadaverous man in his thirties. The sheriff of Butte City had an underslung jaw, heavy brows, and a handlebar mustache. Cradled in his hands was a shotgun, and pinned on his narrow chest was a tarnished badge.

"Hello, Sheriff," Clint said. "I've been wondering when we'd meet. I passed by your office a couple of times, but it seems that you were gone all day. I would have thought that your services would have been especially important given all the celebrating going on in Butte City."

"I had some important trouble east of town. A few horses were stolen by them damned murderin' Ute Indians."

"Is that a fact?" Clint started to lower his hands. "I guess you . . ."

"Keep 'em high!" the sheriff yelled. "Gunsmith, I don't care if you're Wyatt Earp and Wild Bill Hickok all rolled into one! This scattergun says that I can blow your head off."

The miners standing near Clint parted like the Red Sea. They hugged the walls, some even electing to crouch on the floor behind the chairs and tables.

"Take it easy, Sheriff. You're making everyone in this saloon real nervous."

"They needn't be," Denton said. "They elected me, and I'm here to serve and protect them."

"You got a dangerous way of protecting," Clint said, taking the sheriff's measure and not liking his read.

The Gunsmith had faced a lot of men and he could sense a bluff every time. But there was no bluff in Sheriff Denton. Only a dangerous cockiness. Right now, the sheriff's eyes were challenging him

AMBUSH MOON 49

to reach for his six-gun. Clint knew that he was a dead man if he made a play for his gun and that he had to defuse the situation before the sheriff did something crazy, like killing him without any provocation.

"I don't know why you are so set on arresting me," Clint said with a disarming smile. "You see, Sheriff, what you might not understand is that someone tried to gun me down a few hours ago and shot Thelma Boren instead. It would seem to me that—"

"You and Thelma are charged with intent to commit murder against Mr. Henry Reed! I saw his face and saw what Thelma did to him with that frying pan."

"He got what he deserved," Clint said, trying to keep the heat out of his voice. "And as for Luke, he waded into me first and deserved what he got just like Henry. He swore to get even against me and that's why Thelma is in the doctor's office fighting for her life."

"Why don't you listen to the man?" the gambler said. "Everyone knows how goddamn mean Henry and Luke get when they've been hitting the bottle."

"Shut up!" Denton hissed. "I didn't ask for any of your mouth. Lincoln, you stay out of this, or I'll see you are driven out of Butte City first thing tomorrow morning."

Lincoln's jaw muscles corded, but he managed to swallow an angry reply.

Sheriff Denton's eyes swung back to the Gunsmith. "You professional killers have to learn that you can't just ride into a town and start buffaloing and beatin' hell outta its honest and respectable citizens."

"Sheriff, why are you acting like this?" Clint asked. "Are you up for reelection? Is that why you're putting on this big show for the folks? Are you making a fool out of yourself just to impress them?"

A ripple of laughter circled the roomful of miners. There was also a good deal of snickering.

The sheriff's face reddened with anger. "You're pushin' your luck, Gunsmith. In less than it takes for you to blink your eye, I'd be famous if you'd decide to go for that gun on your hip. I'd be . . ."

"Sheriff Denton!" Lincoln exploded. "If you're going to arrest this man, then do it. But nobody is going to allow you to just goad him into being murdered."

The shotgun moved an inch in the gambler's direction. "I warned you to shut up!"

The gambler drew a cigar from his coat pocket. His hand was rock steady as he lit the match, then blew a cloud of smoke at the sheriff, indicating his cool derision. "If you open fire with that scattergun, you might kill a few of us by accident. And sheriff or not, you'd be lynched by the survivors."

Denton surveyed the now hostile crowd. He could see the truth of the gambler's words. "I'm just trying to do my job. This man is under arrest and . . ."

The sheriff's words died on his lips because, in the moment that he had surveyed the crowd, Clint's hand had flashed to the gun on his hip. Now, it was pointed at the sheriff.

"A standoff," the Gunsmith announced. "You got a tough decision to make, Sheriff Denton. Either we drop this foolishness, or we'll probably both die. Which is it going to be?"

"You could miss," Denton whispered nervously. "I damn sure won't with my twin shotgun barrels."

"I won't miss," the Gunsmith said. "Bet on it."

Denton gulped. The shotgun began to shake in his hands while the Colt in the Gunsmith's fist was steady. At this point, it was anyone's guess what the sheriff would do next. Clearly, he was proud and foolish, but now the Gunsmith saw the effect of fear as it corroded his resolve.

"What are you going to do now?" Clint asked almost matter-of-factly.

"Well . . . well," Denton stammered, "you can't just ride into my town and beat people up!"

"It was Luke and Henry against me and Thelma," Clint said in a low, hard voice. "The only thing that makes a difference is that Thelma decided to use a frying pan instead of her fists."

"She shouldn't have hit him so damned hard! You can kill a man with a heavy frying pan," the sheriff said with exasperation. "I took the pan as evidence."

"As evidence?"

"Sure! If Henry died, it would be a murder weapon."

The crowd snickered, some laughed outright, and Lincoln smiled with more pity than warmth. "Hell, Sheriff, quit being an ass and leave us alone. Everyone in Butte City knows that Thelma was afraid of Henry and about to quit that job as soon as she could find a better one. I'll bet tonight's winnings that most of us think that Henry got exactly what he deserved."

"Sure he did!" a miner exclaimed. "Thelma is a damned fine woman. If she brained Henry, then he needed to be brained. That's the way I see it."

"Me too!" another and then another miner shouted.

Completely routed by the saloon full of miners, Sheriff Denton was reduced to a pitiful attempt to save face. "I won't stand for any vigilante justice! If Luke is the one who shot Thelma, *I'll* arrest him!"

"Sure," Clint said agreeably. "I'd be happy to have you ride out with me to the Rocking Horse Ranch."

Denton leapt at the chance to escape the hostile crowd. "Come on then!" he shouted. "I'm not going to wait around for you to get ready."

"I need the loan of a horse," Clint said loud enough for everyone to hear. "Mine has pulled up lame."

"I've got a pretty nice sorrel gelding over at Bud York's stable that you can borrow," the gambler said. "But if you lame him too, you're obligated to buy him for fifty dollars."

"Fair enough." Clint didn't see any point in worrying about the fact that he was dead broke. He turned to the sheriff. "Is your horse saddled yet?"

"No, but I'm real fast."

"I can see that you are also mighty fast to jump into hot water," Clint replied with a straight face that brought chuckles from everyone. "I'll meet you out in front in a half hour. How about that?"

"Don't be a damned minute late!" Denton stormed as he whirled and stalked out the door amid a chorus of laughter.

When the sheriff was gone, Clint holstered his six-gun. "I want to thank you all for not letting that man ramrod me into his jail. The last thing you'll ever see me do is try and live by my reputation or throw my weight around. It isn't my style. But catching a woman-shooter is something that I can't let pass. That's why I'm going after Luke."

"There's a pack of hard men out at the Rocking Horse Ranch," Lincoln said. "You might just be jumping from the frying pan into the fire, so to speak."

"Thanks for the warning," Clint said to the young gambler.

Lincoln smiled. "Like most everyone else in this town, I have a special fondness for Thelma. If Luke is the man that shot her, I hope you save the taxpayers their money and finish the bastard off proper."

"I'll keep that in mind."

Lincoln stepped over to a gambling table and swept off his stack of poker chips. He stuffed them into his pocket and said, "Maybe I'll poke along with you over to Bud's livery."

"I can find your horse."

"Why go to the trouble? I just want to make sure that you get the right sorrel gelding. Otherwise, that fool Denton will embarrass himself again by trying to arrest you for stealing a stranger's horse."

That brought a laugh from the Gunsmith. He stuck out his hand and said, "I owe you."

"No you don't," the gambler said. "The way that I see it, I owe *you*."

"How do you figure?"

"Well," Lincoln said, "before you came to Butte City, I was the biggest thorn in Sheriff Denton's side. Now, you've definitely taken my place. So you see, I'm the one that owes the thanks."

Clint just shrugged his shoulders and led the way outdoors as he and the gambler angled across the dark street toward the livery.

SIX

Sheriff Denton was visibly upset as they rode north out of Butte City. The stars were shining bright and there was a big, yellow moon so that it was easy to see.

"When we get to the ranch, I'll hail them boys," the sheriff said. "They're a mite quick to take action and the last thing we want to do is spook 'em into opening up on us with their guns."

"I disagree about hailing them," Clint said. "What I intend to do is catch them while they're still asleep. That way, if Luke is at the ranch, they haven't got time to either protect or hide him."

"Now listen here!" the sheriff stormed. "In case you're forgettin', I'm the one in charge."

"You might be wearing the badge," Clint said, "but I won't risk my life needlessly because of your foolishness. So I'm going in under the cover of darkness and without warning. And if you try and foul me up, I swear that it'll go hard for you, Sheriff."

Denton stared at him. "Are you threatening an officer of the law?"

"I guess I am," Clint said, pushing his horse into an easy gallop.

Denton almost reined his horse around and headed back to town. Clint could feel the man's indecision and it occurred to him that the sheriff might actually try to shoot him in the back. But Denton hadn't the nerve.

"Hey, wait for me, damn you!"

Clint reined up and waited. "So," he said, not cutting the man any slack, "we're going to do it my way, right?"

"What am I supposed to do while you're sneaking up on these innocent boys?"

"You can hold our horses," Clint said, putting his heels to the sorrel and riding on.

Denton didn't speak to him all the rest of the way out to the Rocking Horse. The man brooded and fussed.

"That's it," Denton growled as they neared the ranch. "But I'm warning you that this is not the way to do things."

"Do I have to worry about any ranch dogs?"

"No. But you can bet they're light sleepers and quick on the trigger. It won't be their fault if they shoot you down in the dark. You're just an ordinary citizen now, Adams. They'll think you are up to no damn good. Men got a right to protect themselves from skulkers."

"I'll keep that in mind," Clint said, surveying the moonlit landscape and deciding that this was about as far as he dared to ride in on the decrepit ranch house, barn, and some pole corrals filled with horses.

Clint had a feeling that moonlight was very, very kind to the Rocking Horse Ranch headquarters.

"What are you going to do now?"

"I guess this is good enough," Clint said, dismounting and handing his reins to the sheriff. "All you have to do is just relax and keep quiet."

"I should be the one going in, not you."

"Perhaps," Clint agreed, "but let's just forget about playing roles. If I find Luke in there, I'll sing out and you can make the arrest. All right?"

"What's going to happen is that them boys are going to riddle you with bullets. And it'll serve you right for not doing things my way."

Clint clamped his mouth shut. There was no sense in trying to placate this fool. So without further discussion, he headed across the open ground toward the ranch house. The stars were already starting to fade, and Clint guessed the first light of day would soon begin to brighten the eastern horizon.

It was his habit never to approach a house or dwelling straight into the doorway. That being the case, he angled across the yard. When he was within about seventy feet of the house, he drew his six-gun and cocked back the hammer.

That was a big mistake. A huge, wolf-like dog awakened to the slight and unnatural sound. The ferocious animal had been sleeping alongside the house in the darkest shadows so that Clint did not see it until the beast was already up and charging with a rumble in its throat.

Like most lawmen, Clint had already been attacked and bitten. That was why he had specifically asked Denton if there was a ranch dog. And now, as the huge animal closed the distance between them with its fangs bared, the Gunsmith could see that it was going to leap for his throat. This was no mere snapper and biter, this was a man-killer.

Clint drew his six-gun, reversed his grip, and braced himself for the attack. He could have shot the beast, but that would have awakened everyone, and since the dog had not barked, he still had hopes of catching the ranch house by surprise. When the animal leapt off its feet, Clint aimed the butt of his gun at the animal's head and slashed downward with all his might. The butt of the six-gun struck the beast, but not between the eyes. Instead the gun butt hit the dog across the top of its long snout.

The beast's rumbling changed to a howl of pain. Clint fell backward as the animal's momentum carried it over him. Clint whirled around, and the dog attacked again. This time, the Gunsmith could see nothing else to do but shoot the vicious animal before it buried its fangs into his flesh.

Clint fired once, and the dog yipped and struck the ground, twitching and biting at the dirt. The Gunsmith heard the sound of yelling inside the ranch house. He jumped toward the wall of the cabin and flattened against its rough surface, listening to furniture being knocked over in the general confusion he'd created.

"Who's there?" a voice called from inside the ranch house. "Dammit, who is there?"

"It's Sheriff Denton and the Gunsmith!"

Clint swore under his breath. He moved to the front corner of the house and yelled, "I shot your dog! I'm looking to bring Luke Bradley to justice for shooting Miss Thelma Boren."

There was a rush of whispering and then some argument. Finally, a voice yelled, "Luke ain't here!"

"In that case," the Gunsmith said, "all of you come out with your hands in the air."

"Go to hell!"

Another man with a hoarse voice shouted, "Sheriff Denton, what's going on out there? Did that son of a bitch really shoot my dog?"

"Yeah," Clint said, "and I'll shoot you if you don't come out with your hands up!"

Gunfire erupted from the ranch house. Clint crouched low and moved all the way around the house. There were windows but no doors. When he came around to the other side, he cupped his hands to his mouth and shouted, "Sheriff, tell them to surrender and nobody will get hurt."

There was a long pause and then Denton said, "Boys! It's the Gunsmith. Someone tried to gun him down tonight but shot Thelma instead. I think you'd better come out with your hands up like he wants or some of you are going to get yourselves killed."

Clint waited. He could hear the men inside arguing. After what seemed like a long time, a man shouted, "All right, we're coming out. Tell that crazy bastard not to shoot! We ain't done nothing wrong."

The men trooped out of the ranch house, hands raised shoulder high. There were four of them in various stages of undress.

"Is that every last one of you?" Clint asked, stepping in behind the men.

"That's all of us," a tall, bearded man wearing red flannel long johns said. "Are you really the Gunsmith?"

"I've been called that," Clint admitted. "Lower your hands and turn around to face me."

They turned and Clint said, "I'm hunting Luke. Is he hiding inside?"

The four men exchanged glances, and then the tall one said, "Nope."

"If you're lying," Clint said, "we're going to have big trouble."

"He's not lying!" a red-bearded man growled. "And mister, I don't care who you are—you sure as hell didn't need to shoot my wolf-dog!"

"He had a bad attitude. What'd you do, beat the hell out of him until he became so mean that he'd go for a man's throat?"

"Hell no! I swear that I never laid so much as a switch to him since he was a pup!"

"Bullshit," Clint said, turning back to the cabin's doorway. With his gun in his fist, he stepped up to it, then suddenly threw himself sideways. It was just a sixth sense that warned him that not everyone had exited the cabin. One, maybe two men out of a hundred would have sensed the danger and now it saved the Gunsmith's life.

Three tightly spaced shots blasted out through the doorway. One of the bullets struck the ranch dog's owner. It hit him in the forehead and he collapsed, dead before he struck the ground. Clint dove through the doorway. He struck the floor and rolled, his own gun coming up and dealing death. Muzzle flash matched muzzle flash, and Clint heard a grunt of pain and then the hollow sound of a body striking the plank floor.

The room fell into a hushed, smoky silence. Clint listened for any sign that would tell him the man he'd just shot had merely been wounded and perhaps was faking his death in order to get the Gunsmith to make a fatal sound revealing his position. But the silence deepened, and the Gunsmith could not even hear a man's breathing.

Clint pushed himself to his feet. He reached into his pocket and drew a match. Extending his arm off to one side, then striking it on his thumbnail, Clint looked across the dark interior of the room and saw the body of Luke Bradley. Blood was leaking out of Luke's right eye where the Gunsmith's bullet had entered. The man was still clutching his gun, and there was a dirty bandage wrapped around his chest.

Clint came to his feet. His match burned out and he lit another, then managed to find a lantern. When the room was filled with its light, he took a good look around and saw squalor and more bloodstained bandages.

Holstering his gun, Clint marched outside. He walked up to the tall man and backhanded him across the mouth. The man staggered, then balled his fists and would have jumped at Clint except for the gun that suddenly appeared in his hand.

"You lied to me," Clint said.

"So what?"

"So I broke your lying lips."

Sheriff Denton came galloping up to the ranch house. He took one look at the situation and said, "I think that we all need to just calm down."

"Shut up," the tall man said, wiping his bloody lips. "This is between him and me."

"He's the Gunsmith."

"He's a dead man when we get our hands on guns."

Clint ignored the threat. He said to Denton, "Luke Bradley is inside. I shot him in the head, but he was shot already. You can plainly see that by the bandages."

"That still doesn't prove that he's the man that ambushed you and shot Thelma by mistake last night. Adams, you've still got no evidence!"

"Maybe not the kind that would stand up in a court of law," the Gunsmith said. "But there isn't a doubt in my mind that Luke was the one that shot Thelma."

Clint went over to the sorrel gelding that he had borrowed, but he never turned his back on the men he'd flushed from the ranch house. He mounted the sorrel and studied the men. "I don't know what you birds claim to do for a living, but I'll bet it's illegal."

"Sheriff, he can't threaten us!"

"I say what I want," Clint said. "And I'll tell you this much, the next time we meet, you'd all better be smiling or reaching for your guns. Because from what I can see, you're just a den of thieves."

Clint backed his horse up and then he spun him around and galloped off, leaving Sheriff Denton and the three scantily dressed men standing in the moonlight.

SEVEN

Sheriff Denton overtook the Gunsmith before he reached Butte City. The sun was just coming up, and Clint was not in a very good mood, given that Thelma had been shot the evening before and he'd also been forced to kill Luke Bradley.

The sheriff looked over at Clint. "I don't see how the hell you ever made it as a sheriff the way you act."

"You mean because I killed Luke Bradley without evidence?"

"Exactly!"

The Gunsmith shrugged. "When the man opened fire on me from inside the cabin, what other evidence did I need? He was wounded, and I'd wounded the man who shot Thelma."

Denton frowned. "It still seems to me that you went off half-cocked back there at the ranch. And threatening to shoot those men the next time that you see them was completely uncalled-for. And I told them that!"

Clint looked through Denton. "Did you lead them

to believe that I was bluffing?"

"Well . . . maybe your temper just got the best of your tongue," the sheriff stammered. "That's all that I was saying. I told them to let you cool down for a few days before they come into my town."

The Gunsmith wondered if maybe he ought to just reach out and grab this fool and wring his neck. Deciding that there had been enough killing, Clint curbed his temper. He could see the town just up ahead, bathed in the first rays of the morning sun.

"Sheriff?"

"Yeah?"

"There's something I want to know more about."

Denton looked over at Clint. "Such as?"

"Such as what's behind these full moon killings that your town is so worked up about?"

Denton opened his mouth, then clamped it shut.

"Spit it out!" Clint ordered.

"I got nothing to say!" Denton squirmed in his saddle. "The truth is, no one knows why people are getting ambushed."

"But there must be some connection between the murders. I can't imagine that they are just random killings. That doesn't make sense."

"It does if it's the Ute Indians that are trying to get even with the town."

"What have they got to get even about?"

"Well," the sheriff began, "about thirty years ago, when Butte City was nothing but a trading post, the Utes were pretty upset about the white people moving onto their lands. There was some gold and silver discovered over at Little Peak and then some more along the river just to the north. Pretty quick, there was a gold rush."

"That's bound to happen."

"There was this old Chief Nacota who was the head Ute at the time. He had son named Midan. The kid was about ten years old and the prospectors caught him stealing some flour. Anyway, they almost hanged the boy."

"For stealing some flour?"

"It was a rough and lawless time," Denton said. "But there was this one fella, a big miner named Benson. Anyway, he saved the boy and when the word of what he'd done got back to Nacota, the old chief was so grateful that he asked for a truce between his people and the prospectors."

Clint nodded. He could almost guess the unhappy ending to this story. "So what happened?"

"Nacota came into town with some of his headmen. Benson was there to greet him and from what I hear, the two became fast friends. They smoked a peace pipe and passed the jug around. I guess they passed it around a couple of times too many."

"What do you mean by that?"

"Someone—and nobody agrees who—someone got mad and the first thing you know, the whole bunch of them were fighting. Nacota died of a knife in the belly. Benson was shot to death after he shot the man who knifed the chief. All but one of the Ute headmen were killed along with about a half dozen prospectors. From what I've been able to piece together of the story, it was a real bloodbath."

"I see." Clint frowned. "And on the basis of some

drunken fight that took place thirty years ago, everyone now thinks that the Ute people have finally decided to get even."

"Dammit, it makes sense! It's the only thing that does make sense!"

"Not to me it doesn't."

Denton flushed with anger. "Well, until you come up with some better explanation, I guess that you'd best accept this one."

"Hell," the Gunsmith growled, "have you even gone to speak with the Utes?"

"There aren't a whole hell of a lot of them left. There was this young Chief Ouray who led his band against the army a few years ago and killed an Indian agent named Nathan Meeker and then killed some soldiers sent to capture him. But Ouray died a while back, and the government took away the Utes' land. Sent most of them to a couple of reservations up north of us."

"But not all of them?"

"No," Denton said. "There were a bunch that refused to leave their lands. They splintered into little groups. A few have gone white and moved into the mining towns, but the rest live up in the higher mountains. Those are the ones that we think are doing the killing. And the most common belief is that their leader is Midan."

"I see. And he, of course, would have the motive of revenge for the death of his father, Nacota, along with the other Ute headmen."

"That's the way we see it," the sheriff said. "Doesn't it stand to reason?"

"Maybe," Clint had to reluctantly agree. "Except for the fact that the Utes have to know that they're playing a losing game, that sooner or later, one of them will get caught ambushing people and the whole lot of them will suffer."

Denton scowled and rode along a few minutes before he broke the silence. "Maybe what's left of the Ute people just don't give a damn about what happens to them anymore. Maybe now that they've lost all but a few specks of their land, they're just seeking a way to get back some honor and revenge."

"Maybe," Clint said, though he had his doubts.

"Looks like a lot of folks are up early this morning," the sheriff said, squinting into the morning sun.

"Looks to me like they're working themselves up to no damn good," the Gunsmith replied, seeing a big group of men gathered in front of a wagon upon which a man was standing and exhorting the crowd.

"Do you know the man that's standing up on the wagon?" Clint asked, touching his heels to the sorrel's flanks and setting him into a gallop.

The sheriff pushed his horse forward a little ahead of the sorrel. "That's Moss Taylor. One of the biggest cattlemen in these parts."

"And a rabble-rouser, I'll bet."

Sheriff Denton said nothing but spurred on ahead. When he reined up near the crowd, the sheriff sang out, "What's the trouble, Mr. Taylor?"

Moss Taylor was a big oak tree of a man. Hatless, his hair was thick and silver. He had a huge rack of shoulders and although his spine was bent with age, he still stood well over six feet tall. His face was burned as brown as tobacco, and his nose was bent like the man himself. Clint could see that Moss Taylor must have been a hell of a man in his prime. He still looked capable of whipping a grizzly with a willow switch.

"Damn you, Sheriff!" Taylor shouted over the crowd. "We're about fed up with waiting for action. I'm telling these boys that they need to show some gumption and take matters into their own hands if the law is too damned yellow to do it!"

Sheriff Denton's cheeks reddened with embarrassment. "Now Mr. Taylor," he began, "we can't just go up into those mountains half-cocked. Why, we don't even know how many Utes are off the reservation! Even the Indian agency can't tell us for sure."

"Well, there ain't enough to worry about, and they'll be a whole lot less when these boys get finished with 'em!" the old man bellowed.

Some of the men in the crowd were drunk and working themselves up to get horses and ride. Clint had witnessed this scene more times than he cared to remember. Drunks, guns, and revenge were a deadly mix.

"Denton, you'd better talk some sense into them," Clint warned under his breath. "They're working themselves up to no damned good."

"I know that!" Denton cleared his throat. "Listen everyone, me and the Gunsmith rode out to the Rocking Horse Ranch last night. We had some gun trouble, and I'm here to tell you that it looks like Thelma was ambushed by Luke Bradley. We would have arrested him, but things got a little out of hand."

"What the hell are you saying?" Taylor demanded. "Spit it out plain, dammit!"

"All right," Denton said. "Luke Bradley was already wounded, but now he's dead."

"Dead?" Taylor gaped. "You killed Luke?"

When Denton glanced sideways at the Gunsmith, it was easy to see that the man needed help. Clint figured he could be silent no longer.

"What the sheriff is saying is that I shot Luke Bradley twice. Once last evening when he tried to ambush me and shot Thelma instead. Then I shot him again early this morning when he refused to come out and be arrested."

Moss Taylor swung his big head around and pointed to the doctor's office. "You mean to say that the Utes *didn't* shoot that woman?"

"That's exactly what I'm saying," Clint growled.

"You got any proof?"

"No, but . . ."

"Then mister, you're just farting into a stiff wind! You killed an innocent man."

Clint prodded his horse into the crowd, forcing it to part. He rode right up to the wagon and glared at Taylor, who glared right back down at him.

"Mr. Taylor," Clint began, his words clipped, "I'm telling you that Luke Bradley was the man who shot Thelma. I've been a lawman too damn many years not to be able to put my finger on the real culprit."

"I liked Luke," the old man hissed. "He was wild

and a little hair-triggered, but he wasn't no woman-shooter."

Clint's patience snapped. "Are you going to listen to reason, or am I going to have to climb down from this horse and then yank you the hell off of that wagon!"

Taylor's lips pulled back in a sneer. "Mister, they say that you were a lawman and now you are a famous gunfighter. Well, that don't count for anything with me! I can hire ten men like you and fire 'em all in the same goddamn day!"

Clint had to force himself to remain in his saddle and not go after the old cattleman. He turned to the crowd. "I'm telling all of you that the Ute Indians had *nothing* to do with Thelma's being shot."

"Oh yeah, well what about Abe Long?" another miner demanded. "Who ambushed and killed him?"

"I don't know," Clint admitted. "But that doesn't change the fact that going out to shoot a bunch of Indians makes no damned sense."

"What the hell is all of this to you?" another man shouted. "You're a stranger to this town. You can just ride on and be done with all this trouble."

"I don't plan to ride on," Clint said. "I'm going to stay and make sure that Thelma is all right. And I'm going to open a gunsmithing business, and in between all that, I'm going to try and find out who is *really* ambushing folks during the time of the full moon."

"The hell you say," Moss Taylor rumbled. "The word is that you're just a has-been and an Indian lover."

The Gunsmith started to climb down from the sorrel, planning to climb up on the wagon and show the old man who really was a "has-been," but a calm voice stopped him.

"Why don't you let it ride?" the gambler named Lincoln said. "If you go after the old man, there's some folks in this crowd that will shoot you."

Clint realized that Lincoln was probably telling him the truth. "All right," he said, dismounting and handling the sorrel's reins to his owner. "And thanks for the good advice."

"Think nothing of it," the gambler said. "Only you'd better know that people will be expecting you to come up with the real ambushers pretty damned quick."

Clint started for the doctor's office, intent on seeing how Thelma's recovery was progressing. "I'll do my best," he told Lincoln as he exited the crowd of fools.

EIGHT

"Well hello!" Clint said, forcing cheeriness into his voice as he stepped into Thelma's room. "How are you feeling?"

"Like I've been shot, died, and been buried."

Clint smiled because he could see that she was only halfway serious. "You're going to be just fine in a couple of days. That's a promise."

"Since it's your promise. I'll hold you to it," Thelma said. She lifted her hand, and he came over to take it and sit on the bed. "You look tired."

"I am," he confessed. "The sheriff and I rode out to the Rocking Horse Ranch. I was hoping that I could catch Luke Bradley and whoever else was out there unawares."

"But it didn't work that way."

"No," Clint said. "A damned dog caught me by surprise and woke up everyone in the ranch house. We had a gunfight, and I was forced to kill Luke."

"He deserved to die," Thelma said.

"I know that, but I was hoping that I might get some information out of him about these ambushings. I don't suppose that the doctor told you that a fella named Abe Long was ambushed."

"No, he didn't. Abe was a fine man. I'm very sorry to hear about it. Any idea who shot him?"

"The townspeople are about ready to form a vigilante committee and ride out to attack the Utes."

Thelma's face reflected her concern. "That would be a terrible injustice! Those poor people wouldn't be the ones at fault. You've got to help protect them, Clint."

"I'll do my best. As a matter of fact, after I've gotten a few hours of sleep, I'm going to find a way to go and visit the Ute people. Right now, I'm out on my feet."

"Get your rest. And the person to ask about the Indians is Johnny Irons."

"Irons?"

"That's right. Johnny dresses Indian and I know that he lives with them and has adopted their ways, but he doesn't look like he has a drop of Indian blood in his veins. As a matter of fact, he has blue eyes. I'm sure that he'd do anything to change that."

"I know the type," Clint said. "A lot of the old mountain men married squaws and turned Indian. A few of them even fought the white man when he invaded the Indian lands."

"That's the kind of man that Johnny is," Thelma said. "He wears buckskins and feathers. He has ever since I first laid eyes on him years ago. He doesn't come to town unless he sneaks in on an evening to buy a few things."

"Why?"

"The miners set upon him after all this ambushing

began. They called him a turncoat and an Injun lover. They made his life a misery and he left town."

"They're calling me an Injun lover too," Clint said. "So I can sympathize with Johnny a little on that account."

"He's a good man," Thelma said, "but he's bitter toward the miners and the town. Still, if you explain about the trouble and the threat to the Ute Indians, I'm sure that he will do everything he can to make sure that the vigilantes don't ride against the Ute people."

"Where can I find him?"

"He lives higher in the mountains. I've heard that he has a cabin beside a small lake about fifteen miles north of Butte City."

"I ought to be able to find the place," Clint said.

"It won't be easy. Johnny Irons never has guests from town. The only people who visit him are his Indian friends, and I'm sure that they don't leave a lot of tracks."

"I don't need a lot of tracks," the Gunsmith said. "I'll find Irons and explain the situation to him. If he doesn't want to help me help the Utes, then I'll do what I can without him. Either way, I mean to get to the bottom of this."

"Are you still dead broke?"

The Gunsmith shrugged. "I've been known to have a little more jiggle in my pockets."

"I've some cash in my purse," Thelma said. "You take it and buy whatever you need for this journey to find the Utes."

"I don't feel right about that."

"It's a loan," Thelma said. "From a friend."

Clint nodded. He really did need to provision himself. "Thanks. There's this gambler named Lincoln that loaned me his horse. What do you know about him?"

At the mention of Lincoln's name, Thelma's smile died. "He's quite a man."

"What does that mean?" The Gunsmith could sense that there was a lot that Thelma wasn't saying but, as yet, he could not read between the lines.

"It means that he and I were lovers," Thelma said. "I guess you'd have heard about it sooner or later, the way folks in this town love to gossip."

"So what happened?"

Thelma squeezed his hand. "So what's it to you, Clint? Don't tell me that you're feeling a pang of jealousy!"

"Naw! Forget I even asked."

"It's all right. Lincoln is a hell of a man, but he's secretive. I never could get him to talk about his past. I thought that if he really loved me, he'd be willing to trust that I'd keep his past—no matter what it might be—a secret. But he wouldn't tell me a thing about where he came from or anything."

"There are a lot of men whose past must be a closed chapter," the Gunsmith said. "It's entirely possible that Lincoln has killed a man and is hiding from the law under an alias."

"I realize that," Thelma said, "and I know that I shouldn't have let the man's past come between us, but it did. And the more I thought about it, the bigger an issue it became. Finally, I broke off our relationship. I was afraid that, if we ever married, the day would come when Lincoln's past would catch up with him and ruin our lives."

"I see," Clint replied. "Well, all I know is that he seems different than most of the other people and he's helped me. Maybe he's done it for you, Thelma."

"I don't think so, though the idea is flattering." Thelma frowned. "Clint, don't put too much trust in Lincoln or anyone else in Butte City."

"Except for you."

She smiled, but a little sadly. "I don't even entirely trust myself, so why should you?"

He leaned down and kissed her on the lips, then stepped back. "I trust you completely, Thelma. When the day comes that I can't trust anyone, then that's the day I'll feel like maybe I've lived too long."

"Be careful!"

"I will," he promised before reaching for her purse and extracting a sheaf of greenbacks. "And I'll find this Johnny Irons and then have a talk with the Ute people. Maybe one of their leaders will consent to riding into Butte City and telling the townsfolk that their fears are completely unfounded."

"I'm not sure that they would believe an Indian."

"Maybe not," the Gunsmith conceded, "but for right now, it's the only thing that I can think of to do."

Clint left Thelma and went to the hotel. He was so tired that he didn't even kick off his boots before stretching out on the bed. He closed his eyes and didn't awaken until noon. Feeling somewhat refreshed, he headed for the Palace Saloon to thank

Lincoln for the use of his horse and to see if the man was willing to let him ride the sorrel in search of Johnny Irons.

"You're welcome to the horse," Lincoln said, "although I'll still expect fifty dollars if he's lamed or lost."

"That's more than fair and agreeable," Clint said, extending his hand. "And thanks!"

The gambler shook his hand, then said, "How's Thelma feeling today?"

"She's feeling much better." Clint paused. "Why don't you go pay her a visit? I'm sure she'd like to see you."

"I don't think so," Lincoln said. "She made it plain a few years ago that she didn't want to see me again."

"Things change," Clint suggested.

"And some things never change." Lincoln shook his head. "No, sir, Thelma is one hell of a woman. She deserves the best and that isn't me."

"Maybe you're being a little hard on yourself. I'm sure that you're not a saint, but who is among us?"

Lincoln shifted uncomfortably, then quickly changed the subject. "By the way, how are you going to find Johnny Irons?"

"Thelma gave me some rough directions. Maybe you could give me some better ones?"

"Nope," Lincoln said quickly. "I've only seen Irons a couple of times. He stays as far away from white people as he can, and you'd best not be expecting him to welcome you with open arms."

"I don't," Clint said. "But I hope that he'll at least

understand why it's important to take me to meet the Ute people."

Lincoln shrugged. "Maybe he will. I couldn't say."

"Well," Clint said, "thanks again for the use of your horse. I'll take good care of the animal and, hopefully, my gelding will be fit to ride soon."

"Sure."

Clint left the saloon and went back to the livery where he explained his plans to Bud York. The liveryman listened carefully, but after Clint was finished, he didn't seem too optimistic. "Hell, as spooked as Johnny Irons has become these days, he might even ambush you if you get too close to his cabin."

"I'll keep my eyes open and my gun loose. Thelma gave me some rough directions, saying that Irons lives about fifteen miles north of town in a cabin by some lake. Does that sound about right?"

"I'd say it was closer to twenty miles or more. Your best bet would be to ride north and when you see a pair of rocky twin peaks, you sort of angle up between them. My understanding is that there is a small lake hidden in the trees and that's where Irons's cabin is resting."

"Thanks."

"Be careful," Bud said. "After the miners beat the hell out of Johnny, he changed. Before that, he was just standoffish. Now, he's real hostile to whites."

"That's not too hard to understand," Clint said. "And I will be careful."

The Gunsmith rode out of the livery, then stopped at a general store where he bought food and another box of ammunition. With his bedroll and an oilskin slicker tied behind his saddle, he rode out of Butte City determined to find Johnny Irons and get to the bottom of this mystery.

The country was green and pretty, and the sorrel was still plenty eager to travel. Clint felt better after his nap, and everything would have been fine except that a summer rain squall caught him about five miles out of town. It was the kind of quick but violent storm that often drenched the Rocky Mountains. For a few minutes, the rain was so heavy that Clint was forced to take shelter in the pines. He dismounted and pulled on his slicker while holding the sorrel.

Within thirty minutes, the squall passed on to the south and the sun came out so warm and bright that it steamed the trees and rocks. Overhead, two golden eagles appeared and began to soar on the updrafts, and all around him freshets of water rushed down the mountainside to join streams which formed rivers.

When the Gunsmith thought about the heat of the Sonoran Desert that he had recently escaped, he was filled with gratitude. He breathed in the scent of pine and was thankful just to be alive and healthy.

By late afternoon, he was within striking distance of the twin peaks and riding up a steep mountain trail. The air was growing chill, and he saw a herd of deer grazing a meadow about a quarter mile away. When they heard the sound of the sorrel's shod hooves striking shale stone, their heads lifted and they studied horse and rider warily for several long minutes. Apparently deciding that the Gunsmith was too far away to pose a threat, they resumed their grazing.

But just a few minutes later, for no apparent reason that Clint could see, the deer again lifted their heads, and a moment later, the entire herd took flight and disappeared into the trees. That told the Gunsmith that something or someone else very threatening was on this mountainside and closer to the meadow and therefore more of a danger.

Clint continued up the steep trail, but now he no longer was admiring the sky, the forest, and the magnificent vistas that presented themselves in almost every direction. He had a sense that someone was watching him, perhaps even stalking him.

The Gunsmith topped a ridge line and reined in his sorrel, which was puffing for breath in the thin mountain air. The horse was covered with sweat and the air was turning chill, so Clint dismounted and loosened the cinch. He also slipped his Winchester out of the saddle boot and, after tying the panting sorrel, moved into a pile of granite rocks and waited to see if he was actually being followed.

He waited until the light was beginning to fade and then he saw a man sneaking up along his back trail. The Gunsmith took one look at the tall, lean, buckskin-clad figure in the fading light of day and knew that he was watching Johnny Irons and that the man was carrying a Sharps hunting rifle.

NINE

Clint stepped out from behind the rocks so that Johnny could see him clearly.

"I come as a friend!" Clint bellowed, no longer able to see the man. "Johnny Irons! I come to help the Ute people!"

Clint's voice echoed up and down the mountain slope then faded away into oblivion. There was no answer; the only sounds that the Gunsmith could hear were the nervous stamping of his horse's hooves and the chatter of the aspen leaves as they brushed against each other in the wind.

What to do? Clint scowled and walked slowly back to his horse. If Johnny Irons would not come out of hiding, then Clint supposed he would have to draw the man out. The only way that was possible was for him to locate Johnny's cabin.

The Gunsmith led his horse through the aspen and when he was sure that they blocked him from Johnny's rifle, he remounted his horse and sent him into a trot on up the mountain. There was no doubt in Clint's mind that the twin peaks that loomed overhead were the ones that served to cradle an

AMBUSH MOON

alpine lake. Once he found the lake, Clint knew that he would find the cabin.

It took him an hour to locate Johnny's cabin. It was nestled into a jumble of boulders and manzanita brush so that it was almost invisible. Furthermore, Johnny had apparently never ridden or even hiked directly up from the alpine lake nor had any of his Ute friends so that there was no visible trail to follow. It was very clear to the Gunsmith that Johnny Irons had taken great care to conceal his cabin.

Clint led his horse into the thickets and unsaddled the weary animal. Then he went into the cabin and had a good look about the place. The small, one-room cabin was surprisingly neat and tidy. Along one wall was a set of bunk beds with thin pallets of pine needles covered by a pair of heavy silver-tipped grizzly bearskins. The bears must have been immense, and Clint wondered if Johnny had killed them both with the same Sharps buffalo rifle that he'd seen him with earlier.

There were many furs hanging from the cabin's rafters and a stone fireplace with a hearth. There were no windows, only a large hole covered by what appeared to be a cowhide.

Clint went over to the wall and removed another heavy hunting rifle, this one a .44 caliber, fifteen-shot Henry with its distinctive shiny brass breech. It was an older weapon, and the lever action was badly out of adjustment. Clint hefted the weapon and wished he had his gunsmithing tools, because he could have repaired the Henry in about five minutes.

Replacing the rifle on the wall, Clint went back to the cabin door but was careful not to expose himself as a clear target.

"Johnny!" he shouted down at the placid lake. "I know you're coming. I'm a gunsmith! I can fix that Henry rifle of yours, and I can help the Ute people!"

A crashing boom and a puff of white smoke erupted from the trees, and a heavy slug buried itself into the door frame. Splinters flew in all directions and one of them lanced into the Gunsmith's left forearm. He ducked back into the cabin, clenching the arm and gritting with pain. It seemed that Johnny was an extremely suspicious man.

Clint removed his bandanna and wrapped it around his forearm to staunch the bleeding. Later he would have to remove the large pine splinter, but right now all his attention was needed in order to survive. Clint drew his six-gun and hunkered down to wait. Johnny would have to come to the cabin in order to dislodge him, and then the odds would be on Clint's side.

The sun slipped behind the western peaks, and shadows raced swiftly across the lake below. Cold wind began to shiver the pines, and Clint sat motionless just inside the door, knowing that, sooner or later, Johnny would come.

Sometime deep in the night, Clint's head snapped up suddenly and he saw Johnny's dark form block out the starlight as he merged into the open doorway. Clint lashed out with his boot, striking Johnny Irons hard against the side of his knee. Johnny grunted in pain and tried to bring his heavy rifle to bear on Clint, but the Gunsmith kicked him a second time and he went down, the Sharps expelling a harmless bullet into the side of the cabin. Clint attacked before Johnny could recover.

He balled his fists and punched Johnny twice in the face, then he grabbed the man by the neck in a vise-like grip and said, "Goddamn you, I said that I was a friend! Quit trying to kill me and show some good sense before I have no choice but to throttle you to death!"

Johnny quit struggling and grated, "Who are you?"

"My name is Clint Adams. I volunteered to come up here and try and find out who is ambushing people down in Butte City. They think that it's the Ute Indians."

Johnny choked and tore Clint's fingers from his throat. "It's not the Utes!"

"Who is it then? You?"

"No."

"Then who is ambushing people during the full of the moon?"

"Get off me and get out of my place."

"Not until you answer my questions," Clint growled, rolling off Johnny but drawing his six-gun and jabbing it hard against the man's chest. "Put your hands over your head and come outside where I can see you and we can talk."

Johnny muttered something that Clint chose to ignore, but he came outside. "Sit down against the cabin, legs crossed and hands on your knees."

When Johnny complied, Clint took a good look at the man. Johnny was the kind that deserved a second look. He was large, but well past his prime as evidenced by his wild mane of silver hair. He was wearing buckskins and a coonskin hat, just like the old-time mountain men. His moccasins were decorated with colorful beads, and his face was lean, dark, and shaped like a slice of pumpkin pie.

"If you think I'm the one that has been ambushing them damned whites during the full of the moon, why don't you just shoot me and be done with it?"

"Because I'm not a cold-blooded killer," the Gunsmith replied. "And besides, before I'd shoot you, I'd have to hear a reasonable motive."

"I hate white people," Johnny said. "That ought to be motive enough."

"It isn't," Clint replied. "We all hate certain people, but that doesn't mean we ambush them. Besides, you were carrying a hunting rifle and that weapon on the wall is broken. The men ambushed down in Butte City were shot by a smaller caliber weapon."

"How do you know that?"

"Like I said, I'm a gunsmith by trade."

"I'll bet," Johnny said cryptically. "You're a hired gun sent up here by them folks to kill me and any stray Ute Indians that you can draw a bead upon."

"You can think what you will," Clint said. "But that just isn't true. I told the people down there that it was preposterous that the Utes would be killing during a full moon to satisfy some kind of tribal ritual."

Johnny barked a laugh. "Oh yeah? Well, what did you tell them?"

"That I'd come up here and talk to you. They said that you'd have some answers."

"They were wrong," Johnny spat. "I have no answers for you or any other white man."

Clint sat back on his heels and scowled. He had been a law officer too long not to have become a pretty fair judge of men. And it was clear to him that there was no point in trying to intimidate or threaten Johnny Irons. The man was filled with pure hatred for the whites and it was obvious that he'd rather die than cooperate.

"Johnny, how come you hate white people so much?"

"I guess that's none of your damned business."

"Maybe and maybe not," Clint said, lowering the hammer of his six-gun. "It's clear that you won't help me."

"That's right." Johnny's eyes narrowed. "In fact, I'll kill you if I get the chance."

"That wouldn't be very smart."

Johnny blinked because Clint's remark had thrown him off balance. "Why not?"

"It's like I said, I came up here to find the *real* ambushers. I've no desire to see a bunch of drunken fools ride out of Butte City and go Indian hunting."

"Why should you give a damn about the Utes?"

"The Indians have gotten a bad shake. More than that, I've been a lawman most of my adult life, and I take some pride in seeing that justice is carried out and that the guilty are caught and punished."

"But you have no idea who the guilty are."

"That's right," Clint admitted. "I'm a newcomer to Butte City and this part of the country. I walked into something that smells bad and needs to be put right."

Johnny scoffed with derision. "Sure, you're just a real crusader going from town to town trying to right the West's wrongs."

Clint had had enough of this man's cynicism. "You're wasting my time," he said, holstering his gun. "I'll be leaving, and if you try and ambush me again, I'll kill you."

"We'll see."

Clint backed away. "I'm going to either have to find the Utes and see if they'll help clear themselves or . . ."

"They don't need to clear themselves!" Johnny yelled. "Because they're not guilty of any crime. It's the damned white men who have broken all the treaties and taken their lands. Who have fouled the rivers and cut down the forests."

"Yeah," Clint said. "But like it or not, the white people are calling the shots now, Johnny. And so the Indians can either try and clear their names and make people see their point of view so that justice might be served, or they can continue to fight until they are all gone. Even the Apaches have seen the wisdom of trying to come to peace with the whites. I think it's time people like you did the same."

Clint backed off and went around behind the cabin to where his sorrel was waiting. Keeping one eye on the cabin and his right hand as close as possible to his Colt, the Gunsmith quickly saddled his horse. He was about to remount and ride away when Johnny appeared.

"Wait. You don't have any idea where the Utes are right now."

"No, but I could find them."

Johnny stared at him and then a faint smile appeared on his lips. "You got a lot of confidence, don't you?"

"About some things."

Johnny toed the earth with his moccasin. "I'll take you to Midan," he said at last. "I don't know if he will even speak to you. In fact, he might even lift your hair."

Johnny barked a laugh. "You still of a mind to go Ute hunting, mister lawman?"

"I am."

"All right then," Johnny said, his smile vanishing. "First we eat. In the morning, we go."

Clint nodded. It was late and his horse was about played out. Clint unsaddled once again and then he tied the horse off in the thickets. "You got any grass hay or grain?"

"There's some corn in a gunnysack in that lean-to," Johnny said. "But that horse is too damned fat anyway."

Clint disagreed. But then, most Indian ponies were thin except in the spring and the summer when the grass was plentiful. The rest of the year, they were half-starved and often reduced to staying alive by chewing the bark off the cottonwood trees.

When Clint had finished feeding the hungry sorrel a couple of pounds of dried corn, he went into the cabin to see Johnny lighting a fire.

"Sit down," Johnny said. "You like bear meat?"

It was not exactly Clint's favorite, but he was hungry enough to eat raw porcupine so he nodded.

"Good," Johnny said. He drew a big hunting knife from his belt, and Clint's hand automatically flashed to his gun.

Johnny laughed. "Say, you are a suspicious man! You must have thought I was going to throw this knife at you!"

"The thought did flash through my mind."

"Ha! I could have killed you a couple of times since you went out to saddle that fat horse of yours. But I didn't. Now, you take that knife and go around behind the cabin. Walk about fifty feet into the trees and you'll see a bear carcass hanging by a rope. Got a white man's pulley rigged up so that the wild animals can't get to the meat. You let it down, cut us some bear meat, and bring it back here for cookin'."

"All right."

But at the door, the Gunsmith stopped and looked back at Johnny Irons. "Why do you hate white men so much?"

Without turning away from the fire he was stoking, Johnny growled, "You already asked me that once and I told you it was none of your damned business. I'm tellin' you the same thing now."

"Sure," Clint said. "Then tell me about Midan."

Now Johnny turned to look directly at Clint. "If Midan doesn't kill you the second he lays his eyes on you, maybe you'll have time to ask him to talk about hisself."

"Yeah, maybe," Clint said, turning away and heading around behind the cabin to find the bear carcass.

TEN

"Is this grizzly?" Clint asked, chewing on what he was sure was the toughest and gamiest piece of meat he'd ever tried to swallow.

"Nope. Black bear. Most of the grizzly are about hunted out in these mountains. There are still some up in the higher country, but I wouldn't kill another one. Too damn few left. White men will get the last."

"I suppose," Clint said. "Were you once a trapper or a hunter?"

"I done both."

"But not as a profession?"

Johnny eyed him over the piece of dripping meat he held in his hands. "I think you ask too damn many questions."

"It's the only way I know how to learn what's necessary."

Johnny thought about that for a minute as he chewed the tough bear meat. Then, he raised his head and glared at Clint. "When I first come to this country, it was with gold fever runnin' like a fire through my veins. I was as crazy as any of them that ever came into this country. I fought and clawed at the rocks and the stream and I found me the gold. I became a rich man for a time, I surely did."

"No one told me that down in Butte City."

Johnny scoffed. "Most of them that's still there are worthless as tits on a boar bear. There's only a few of us old-timers left; the best of us have died."

"So you found gold," Clint said, sensing that Johnny might finally open up a crack and reveal something of his past and the reason for his present hatred. "What happened to it?"

"Oh, I spent it," Johnny said. "I spent it on doodads and jingles. I bought horses, good liquor, a big house, and a lot of fast women."

"I see. And you went broke?"

"Yeah. I figured that, if I could find me one fortune, I could find another."

"A mistake, I'd guess."

"No," Johnny said, "I was right. After I pretty near ruined my health and spent all my money, I came right back into these mountains and started prospecting again. Took me six months the second time, but I finally found a promisin' vein of pure silver."

"Silver?"

"Yep. It was shinin' like a string of pearls laid out and washed clean. I found it after three days of the hardest damned rain that I ever did see. It was rainin' so hard that it near to stripped the hide off'n my horse! But it washed away the side of a mountain and there was this vein of silver. My Gawd, when I first saw it I couldn't believe my eyes.

I thought it was quartz rock, but it wasn't. It was the most beautiful thing you ever laid eyes upon. Thick as a gawddamn horse."

Johnny looked into the fire, bear grease leaking from the corners of his mouth and running into his beard. He was a strange man, Clint thought, hard and hateful but also somehow vulnerable. Clint thought that Johnny had a sense of honor and could be trusted. If he decided to kill you, he would give a fair warning first. At least, that was Clint's strong impression as he watched the man chew and stare like a lost soul into the fire.

"So what happened to the vein of pure silver as thick as a gawddamn horse?"

"Well, I knew that I had to figure out some way to get that silver out of the mountain before anyone could find it. You see, people will shoot you dead for a damned dollar. I knew that someone would ambush me for that silver while I was working the face of that bald mountainside and there was just no way to protect myself."

"Why didn't you decide to hire a couple of riflemen to guard you?"

"Hell," Johnny scoffed, "they'd have shot me too!"

"I see."

Johnny sighed. "I thought about it for a couple of days, and then I decided to dig the vein out myself. Maybe a couple tons of it and haul the silver off closer to town, then go up on top of that bald mountainside and cut some trees down and roll 'em over the top of the vein so it couldn't be seen by anyone."

"You were going to fill in your drift and cover it up."

"That's right." Johnny chuckled. "I figured that the vein would be like a cache. I could just go back to it every time I lost my fortune and dig out another couple of tons. That way, I'd always be rich."

"I see." Clint did not think the plan very practical, but he saw no reason to say so.

"Anyway, I began to work on that big old vein of pure silver. I worked from sunrise until sunset digging out silver and haulin' it down into the trees and hiding it. Instead of gold fever, I had silver fever and it was just as bad. You see, the fever is *greed*. Gold, silver, copper, diamonds, greenbacks. It's all the same, and it's a poison to the soul."

Clint nodded. Johnny had the basics right. "I agree."

"Well, sir, winter came early that year and I had me only a ton dug out when the first big storm hit these mountains. I wasn't in none too good a shape. I was worked down to the bone and half crazy with silver fever. And instead of just quittin' and takin' what I had to town, I kept working. Worked right through that blizzard and froze to death."

"What?"

"Froze to death! The Ute Indians, they musta been watchin' me for a long time. And when they saw me freeze solid, they came over and picked me up. Carried me stiff as a twisted tree branch to their camp and they made big medicine on me. Spoke to their spirits."

"And you believe you were dead and that the Indian

medicine and spirits brought you back to life?"

"No question about that," Johnny said, voice ringing with conviction. "My heart was stopped and then it started to beat. My eyes was open, but there was no light, and suddenly, the light poured in from the Great Spirit and my bones that was froze turned warm and blood flowed through my veins."

Johnny winked. "And I had a vision."

"Of what?"

"Can't tell you. I told the Ute medicine man. And I told Midan too. They know, but they're the only ones. After that, what was left of the Ute people knew that I was talkin' true to them. They'd brought me back to life and that made me one with them."

"I see."

"No you don't, white man. You couldn't understand in a hundred years. You don't know a thing about the Indian."

Clint curbed his anger. "I know a few things. I've lived with the Apache and the Paiute. I've fought the Kiowa and I've hunted with the proud Shoshone. What I've learned from all of them is that they respect honesty and bravery."

Johnny stopped chewing the bear meat and spat a piece of gristle or bone into the flames. "Maybe Midan won't shoot you on sight after all."

"I hope that you'll talk him into giving me the chance to help his people."

"The only help they need is just to be left the hell alone."

"That won't happen if I don't find out who is ambushing people during the time of the full moon.

Do you have any idea of anyone who'd do such a thing?"

"No."

Clint sighed with disappointment, for he believed Johnny. "Until I find the ambusher or ambushers, the Ute people will remain the prime suspects. And someday, a crowd of drunken miners and riffraff will come boiling back up into these mountains bent on revenge."

"Then they'll all die," Johnny said flatly. "We'll cut them down like wheat before the sickle's blade."

"But then more will come to avenge those that you cut down. And even if you and the Utes kill them, more will come and finally, you'll all be gone."

"Maybe that is the way it is meant to be," Johnny said with a fatalism that was not uncommon among Indians.

"Can you look into the face of a Ute child and say that? Can you tell a little Ute boy or girl that they were born only to be shot down by crazy whites?"

Johnny choked on his bear meat, then hurled it into the fire. When he turned to face Clint, his hawkish face was twisted with anger and agony. "No, damn you, I couldn't!"

"Then you'd better help me to find the full moon killers, Johnny. You'd better help me before it's too damned late."

Johnny lapsed into a brooding stare as though he could lose himself in the flames. Outside the wind began to stiffen and the branches of pines whipped against the hidden log cabin.

Clint choked down every last bit of bear meat that

he could stomach. He realized that he had to be famished and that he needed this meat, no matter how rank and tough, to keep up his strength for whatever challenges awaited him.

A full belly and the heat of the fire made the Gunsmith's eyelids grow very heavy. He began to nod, then his chin would jerk upward and his eyes would snap open.

"Here," Johnny said, throwing him one of the heavy bearskin robes. "Wrap yourself up in that and go to sleep."

"You're not going to try and cut my throat in the dark, are you?"

"No," Johnny promised. "I'll leave that work to Midan, if he chooses to see your blood."

"How many people does he have left?"

"Go to sleep."

"What happened to your vein of pure silver?"

"None of your damned business!"

"Did the whites ever find it?"

There was a long silence. "No, I cut down them trees up on top and buried it again."

"And that ton of silver that you unearthed before the blizzard. Did you sell it?"

Johnny looked at Clint, and his eyes gleamed in the firelight. "I did," he said. "I used it to buy my adopted Ute people a chance to survive. You see, I bribed politicians, ranchers, and judges. And, just in case they double-crossed my new people, I bought Midan and the Utes plenty of rifles and ammunition."

"You couldn't have bought off all those people and

then had enough left to supply the Ute with rifles and ammunition. Not with just a ton of silver."

In reply, Johnny cackled into the flames, then barked, "So you're smart enough to have been a pretty good lawman, huh?"

Clint wrapped the bearskin around him and closed his eyes. He didn't yet have a clue about who was behind the ambushings, but he'd bet his butt that old Johnny was still mining that pure vein of hidden silver.

ELEVEN

"Wake up, white man," Johnny ordered, prodding Clint with his moccasin. "Ain't no time to sleep like a lady until the damn sun shines."

Clint sat up and rubbed his eyes. Johnny had rebuilt the fire and was crouched before it, rubbing his hands together. In the background, Clint could hear the sound of thunder and lightning. He noticed that Johnny was wearing a buffalo hide coat.

"It is storming?"

"It is for a fact. Bad day to travel. Slick trails, hard for a horse to keep its footing. You better leave that sorrel gelding here and walk."

"No thanks."

Johnny shrugged. "Suit yourself." He lifted a hunk of charred bear meat. "You want another feed?"

"I'll pass."

"Gonna be a long, hard climb."

Clint relented. "All right."

"Here," Johnny said, dropping the sizzling hunk of bear meat on the bearskin robe covering the Gunsmith. "Hog it down and let's get to movin'."

Clint had been so tired the night before that he hadn't even bothered to remove his boots. Now, he sat up and scrubbed his eyes, dearly wishing for a cup of hot coffee to get him started. But there would be no coffee, only the stinking, burning bear meat.

Eat, he told himself, because God only knows when you'll have another chance. Things could and very well might get a whole lot worse before they get better—even if Midan and his people don't kill you.

Clint steeled himself and willed his stomach to accept what it was about to receive. Then, he gingerly picked up the greasy bear meat and chewed himself into wakefulness.

They left the cabin less than thirty minutes later. Clint had a heavy coat and a rain slicker, but it was old and torn. He knew that he'd soon be soaking wet.

"You sure you want to ride?"

"Yeah."

"Trail is steep and narrow."

Clint tugged his hat down. "How far?"

"Can't tell you that. In fact, I'll have to blindfold you a couple hours before we get to Midan's camp."

Clint stifled his rising anger. "I don't see why the deuce that's necessary."

Johnny looked up at him. He was wearing a coonskin cap and he looked like a mountain of moving fur. "You don't understand much of anything about what's been going on around these parts, mister. The truth is that the only way Midan and his people have kept alive is to stay clean away from the white people. To do that, they've got to move their camps plenty often."

Clint supposed this was true. He looked up at the dark clouds, wishing he could detect a sign that the sun was going to break through and that the rain would pass, but he saw nothing that gave him hope.

It had been raining lightly when they'd left the cabin, but as they climbed higher into the storm clouds, the rain intensified until Clint was riding in a cold drenching downpour. As promised, the trail was steep, narrow, and it began to get slick. Clint discovered the gambler's sorrel was not an especially good mountain trail horse. He began to slip and almost fall to his knees and, after each of these episodes, became increasingly reluctant to continue.

"Come on!" Clint urged, wishing like anything that he was riding Duke, his own black gelding. Duke had the agility of a mountain goat and wouldn't have been the least bit fazed or intimidated by this slippery trail.

Clint forced the sorrel ahead, though he had to keep booting the animal in the ribs to keep him moving and not fall too far behind Johnny Irons.

Once, Johnny stopped and waited for him on the trail. When he saw how fearful the gelding was, he said, "You ought to just get off and walk."

"And what would I do with my horse?"

"Unsaddle him and turn him loose."

"Nope," Clint said stubbornly. "I borrowed this horse, and I promised that I'd pay fifty dollars if he was hurt, lost, or killed. I haven't got fifty dollars, and I'm not about to give up the horse."

"Suit yourself," Johnny said, glaring up into the driving rain. "But stubbornness can get a man killed in this hard country."

"I'll remember that," Clint said, feeling the cold rain coursing down his spine into his pants. He'd be lucky if he didn't get pneumonia and die.

The trail degenerated even more as they climbed, using switchbacks that folded back and forth onto themselves. And then, just as Clint had feared and Johnny had prophesied, the sorrel lost his footing and went over the side of the trail. It happened where a rock that formed the base of the trail just oozed out of the mud and went rolling down the mountain. The sorrel, whose weight had been the cause of the rock's dislodgment, followed.

Clint shouted and tried to kick out of his stirrups, but his slicker got tangled up and he felt the sorrel's weight bounce over him. He lost consciousness as he and the terrified animal went rolling down the mountainside into a deep gorge.

When Clint woke up a few seconds later, he was lying pinned under the thrashing sorrel and lying in a freezing stream. The icy water was lapping at his face, and it was a wonder that he had not drowned. He would have already drowned if he and the dying horse had rolled over one more time and ended up a few yards deeper into the water.

Clint struggled weakly to pull himself out from under the horse, but it was hopeless. He thrashed and lost consciousness again for several moments but woke up when the sorrel made one last feeble attempt to rise, then fell back.

"Johnny," Clint called in a voice that he barely recognized. "Johnny!"

Johnny Irons finally reached his side in a shower of gravel. "Well," he said, "good sense tells me that I ought to take your six-gun and use it to put you *and* your poor horse out of your misery."

"Help get him off of me," Clint gritted.

"Why should I?" Johnny squatted on his heels from atop a flat rock and studied the Gunsmith. "Seems to me that you're just another white man. Maybe some better than average, but I don't trust you, and Midan won't either. In fact, I might even be doing you a favor if I put you out of your misery right now."

Clint rolled his head against the flowing water. "How the hell you figure?"

"Midan might torture you to death."

"I'll take my chances!"

The old man sighed and cocked his head like a bird listening for a cricket. "And if I get you outta there, how you gonna travel? Probably got some busted legs or ribs."

"No I don't! I'll travel." In truth, Clint did not know if his bones were broken because he was numb, either from the icy water or from shock.

Johnny spat a stream of tobacco across his rock and then he came to his feet. "All right," he said, wading into the stream and grabbing the sorrel's hind legs. "But this might hurt."

Clint didn't have time to comment. When Johnny rolled the horse's weight off of him for an instant, the Gunsmith tried to pull himself out, but he felt paralyzed. A jolt of raw fear coursed through his veins and made him flail out with his hands and grab a rock, then drag himself free.

Johnny reached down and pulled Clint's six-gun from his holster. He cocked back the hammer and shot the horse between his eyes. The sorrel groaned and quivered, then stiffened and seemed to deflate.

"He's gonna foul the stream, that's for sure," Johnny said, turning away from the horse. "And you're the one that's to blame. You should have turned him loose like I said."

Clint lay staring up at the old man, wondering if Johnny would turn the six-gun on him.

"Stand up, white man."

Clint tried to wiggle his toes, but they wouldn't respond. Using his arms, he pushed himself over onto his belly, still half in and half out of the frigid stream. He tried to stand up, but his legs were things apart from the rest of his body and he toppled helplessly to the rocks.

"Well, sir," Johnny said, "it looks to me like you're done for. You can't even stand, let alone walk outta this here deep gorge. If'n I was you, I'd ask to be shot like that horse."

Clint glared up at the man. "Well," he gritted, "you're *not* me! And I'm not a quitter."

"And I'm no packhorse," Johnny said, bending to untie Clint's saddlebags. "You got anything worth money?"

"No."

"Sure you do! Extra ammunition is always valuable."

As Clint watched helplessly, Johnny removed the box of ammunition and shoved it into his wooly buffalo coat. Then, without a word, he turned and started back up the mountainside.

"What are you going to do?" Clint asked, afraid that he knew the answer.

"I'm going to do the only thing I can and that's save my own self. I might have to hike a couple miles downstream before I can find a trail up and out of this gorge, but that's what I'm fixin' to do."

"What about me?"

"You're a goner," Johnny said without emotion. "You want me to shoot you so you don't suffer, I'll do 'er. If not, then so long. There's no damn way that I can pack you out from down here."

"You could get help."

"Nope."

"The Ute people might help!" Clint shouted in anger and frustration.

"They'd ask me why, and I'd not have an answer," Johnny said, shrugging his shoulders. "That being the case, it makes no sense to ask."

"Dammit!" Clint roared, trying again to stand but failing.

"You can't just walk away and leave me to die."

"Sure I can," Johnny said. "And I am."

With that, Johnny walked away.

Clint pushed himself up on his elbows and shouted, "At least leave me my six-gun!"

Johnny stopped and turned around. "Why? You want to use it on yourself? If you do, then say so and I'll put a quick bullet through your head and keep the gun. If not, why waste a good weapon? After you die, it'd just rust and turn useless. Be no good to anyone."

"You cold-blooded son of a bitch!"

Johnny raised the gun and took careful aim at the Gunsmith. Clint glared at Johnny with defiance. When Johnny fired, Clint was sure it was the last millisecond of his existence, but the bullet just brushed his hair and then ricocheted meanly off a rock.

Johnny chuckled. "I think this damn gun fires a little to the left."

Clint didn't have a reply. So he just hugged the rock and waited for Johnny to correct his own mistake and kill him. Instead, the man turned on his heel, picked up his big hunting rifle, and headed downstream.

The Gunsmith knew it was wasted strength and effort to call after the man. Johnny had little conscience or perhaps no regard for a white man's life. He probably wasn't a killer, but he was a long way from being a hero or a savior.

The hell with him, Clint thought. He possessed a sharp hunting knife and the will to live. He'd find a way to survive. Somehow, he'd get out of this lost mountain gorge and return to civilization. And after that, unless he was paralyzed from the waist down as he was at this very moment, he would return to these mountains, beat Johnny Irons to within an inch of his life, and then find the damn Ute Indians.

TWELVE

It didn't take any genius for Clint to figure out that he had to get moving if he expected to survive. Not only did he have to move, but he had to escape this deep gorge and regain his bearings. But first, he had to merely get upright and then determine the extent of his injuries. If both of his legs were broken . . . well, then he was probably finished and might have been wiser to have allowed Johnny to shoot him as offered.

Clint dragged himself over to a beaver-gnawed stump and leaned heavily against it. He removed his own hunting knife from its sheath and used it to hack a straight branch from part of the fallen tree, then carve a crotch where his armpit would rest. Hopefully, he had at least one good leg and wouldn't need two crutches.

All the time he worked on the crutch, the Gunsmith kept slapping at his thighs and trying to see if he could wiggle his toes. It was not until the crutch was almost ready that he regained feeling in both legs, and that brought a smile to his battered and bruised face despite his desperate circumstances.

With his toes wiggling, Clint tried to bend his knees and climb to his feet but felt a stab of pain.

"Uh-oh," he muttered, using his knife to cut into his pant leg so that he could see the extent of his physical damages.

His left knee was badly swollen and discolored. His right knee was also battered but not so disfigured. Clint tried again to bend the right knee and succeeded, though the effort was painful enough to cause him to groan. Understanding one's personal limitations was part of solving them, and Clint used the stump to haul himself up to his feet. He shoved his crutch under his left armpit, took a deep breath, and then swung forward in an awkward, hopping motion.

He almost lost his balance and toppled back into the freezing stream. Somehow, he regained his balance and steadied himself, then took another tentative and shorter step.

There, that's better.

And it was better. In four or five strides, he learned the hang of it because it was not the first time that he had suffered a leg injury and had been forced to use crutches. Clint figured that he could have progressed nicely along a boardwalk or the flat surface of a city street, but this gorge was tangled with brush and covered with rocks so that the going was slow and difficult. After an hour of concentrated effort following the clearly defined tracks Johnny had left during his own departure, Clint could look back and no longer see the poor dead sorrel.

Thinking about the sorrel brought anger and remorse to the Gunsmith. He should have taken old Johnny's advice and set the animal free. The rain had slackened, but it was still falling and the trails would continue to degenerate. Clint tipped his face back and stared upward into the falling rain. He did not allow himself to think about how desperate his circumstances were, how slim his chances of survival. Instead, he concentrated on using the crutch and taking one small, tentative step at a time.

Finally, he came to the place where Johnny's tracks angled up the side of the gorge. It was a trail, Clint supposed, but not much of one and certainly not enough of one to navigate on a crutch. And yet Clint knew that if he continued down the gorge, he would lose Johnny's trail and die in this huge mountain wilderness. So really, he had no choice but to follow the old man's tracks and hope that they would lead him to the Utes. After that, it was up to the Indians to decide his fate.

Clint eyed the steep, angling game trail that Johnny had used to climb out of this precipitous, inhospitable gorge. He wasn't sure if he could manage it, but he knew that he had no choice but to try. So he unfastened his gun belt and used it to bind the now useless crutch to his body. Taking a deep breath, he attacked the slope on his hands and his good knee.

It was agony. The trail was muddy and oozing rainwater. For every yard that Clint gained in progress, he lost two feet sliding backward. But he kept his head down and continued to crawl and claw at the slope, moving steadily higher. The

AMBUSH MOON

Gunsmith lost all track of time. He vowed that he would escape the gorge or die trying and so he just kept crawling, afraid to look up because it would be too disheartening to measure his poor progress.

It was almost sunset when the sun broke through the clouds and the rain stopped falling. Clint didn't notice anything until he suddenly perceived that he was no longer climbing but resting on flat ground. Then, he raised his head to the setting sun and that was when he realized he was resting at the feet of Johnny Irons and a crowd of Ute Indians. Clint's head snapped up, and he must have been a sight because the Indians were studying him with curiosity and amazement.

"Gunsmith," Johnny said, "you proved to me that you got the will to live. Proved it to my friends too. You've a hell of a lot of guts—for a white man."

"Thanks," Clint said wearily as he unbuckled his gun belt and removed his crutch. He buckled his gun belt on again before he pounded the crutch into the muddy ground and used it to lever himself to his feet.

Clint picked out the man he thought was the chief. "You must be Midan, Chief of the Utes and son of Nacota."

"I am Midan," the grim-faced Indian replied.

Clint judged Midan to be about forty years old. His hair was streaked with silver and there were deep lines etched into his strong face. His eyes had a penetrating quality that was typical of the Utes, and he was dressed in a buffalo robe very much like that which Johnny Irons wore. There was not a trace of jewelry or decoration save a feather in his raven-black hair, and he stood about five foot ten. He was powerfully built and had an air of dignity befitting a chief.

"My name is Clint Adams."

"This I know from Irons. They call you the Gunsmith."

Clint blinked with surprise. "Yeah," he admitted. "I've been called that before."

"You fix guns."

"That's right."

"You fix *our* guns."

"I . . . I'm without my tools." Noting the chief's deepening scowl, Clint quickly added, "But I'd be happy to have a look at them and see what I can do."

This seemed to satisfy Midan and so Clint said, "Did Johnny also tell you the reason for my visit?"

Midan nodded.

"Then," Clint continued, "I hope that you will believe me when I say that I want to clear up the trouble between you and the people of Butte City."

Midan's eyes flicked away to regard his six impassive warriors. He spoke something to them quite rapidly in their language, and the Indians muttered a response that the Gunsmith took as less than favorable.

Midan turned back to Clint. "This thing about the killing of white people during the time of the full moon. Is that about which you speak?"

"Yes."

"We hide from the white people. They are our enemies, but we do not shoot them in the back."

"I believe you."

"Long ago," Midan said, his voice rising with anger, "this was Ute land! Then the white men came and took it from my father's people. They killed him and the good white man named Benson. We trust you no more."

Clint nodded. He was so exhausted from his struggles that he was not sure he could stand like this much longer.

"Chief, if it's all the same to you, could we find a dry place to sit down and talk?"

Midan studied him for a minute, then barked a command. A warrior stepped forward and drew a stone club from his belt. Clint steeled himself, inwardly preparing to die fighting if that was to be his fate.

"Midan! I come as a friend to help you. . . ."

But whatever else Clint might have wanted to say was lost as the warrior's club whistled through the sunset. Clint tried to duck and throw a punch, but his knee betrayed him and he lost his balance. Then, the club smashed against the side of his skull. Clint and his crutch toppled. He struck the earth as the world was filled with an onrushing and absolute darkness.

When the Gunsmith awoke, he was resting in a large wickiup. There was a camp fire blazing, and the room was warm and filled with the scent of unwashed bodies and wet dogs. Clint opened his eyes and tried to gather his wits. It wasn't easy. His head was throbbing where he'd been clubbed. Someone had placed a steaming poultice on his badly injured left knee, which burned like nettles. He could hear the Indians talking in low, measured voices.

Clint lay still for several minutes and then he realized that he was being watched over by a pair of boys both about ten years old. When he forced a smile, the boys called out, and Clint quickly found himself surrounded by curious Utes.

"Hello," he said, pushing up to his elbows and grinning at the old Indians who stared at him.

There was no answer until Johnny Irons squeezed into view and stared down at him. "So," he said, "your brains ain't entirely scrambled."

"No thanks to you."

"How's the knee feelin'?"

"Like it's been spitted over coals."

Johnny barked a laugh. "Hell, white man! Dog Woman is going to have that knee fixed up good as new."

"What about my head?"

"Say the word," Johnny replied, "and she'll put them hot poultices on that lump too."

"No thanks." Clint looked around. "Where's Midan?"

"He's coming. I told him all about the problems down in Butte City. At first, he just wanted to kill you. Now, however, he's willin' to listen."

Johnny scratched his beard. "You sure do owe me your life, Gunsmith."

"Maybe. But if I could have caught up with you on that mountain slope, I'd have just as soon strangled you with my bare hands."

Johnny was about to make some reply when the chief appeared. Immediately, the old Indians parted, and Midan glared down at the Gunsmith with unmistakable dislike and distrust.

"Why do you come in search of Midan?"

"I want to find out who is ambushing down in Butte City. And I want to make those people understand that it is not your Ute people."

"How you do this?"

"I don't exactly know," Clint admitted. "The truth of the fact is that I was sort of hoping you might be able to tell me who might be behind the killings."

"Whites kill each other for no reason. Sometimes gold. Sometimes over a woman. Sometimes drunk. Sometimes sober. No reasons."

Clint nodded; it was a true enough assessment. However, true or not, he needed more help. "I talked to someone who told me about what happened some thirty years ago between the Utes and the prospectors. He told me how your father and a man named Benson were killed."

Midan frowned. "Utes betrayed. Benson betrayed."

"I'm sure they were. But by anyone in particular?"

Midan's eyes narrowed. "Why you ask?"

"I haven't the damnedest idea," Clint admitted. "It's just that I've thought plenty about this, and my mind keeps homing back to that terrible day long ago when your people and those prospectors had a bloodbath. I can't help but think that the present rash of ambushings might somehow be tied in to that."

Midan looked to Johnny Irons, obviously seeking his comment. Johnny cleared his throat and then said, "Midan was only ten years old then. Most everyone that was at that little fight has all died off by now."

"Were you there?"

"I was a boy." Johnny looked into Midan's dark eyes and then turned back to Clint. "Yeah, I was there. I helped Midan escape, as a matter of fact."

"Who else living was there?"

Johnny again looked to Midan, who nodded. "There were a few other youngsters, both Indian and white."

"Anyone else?"

"Yeah," Johnny said. "There was one man that could figure prominently into the puzzle."

"Who is that?"

"Moss Taylor."

"He was there?"

"More than that," Johnny said, "he was up to his neck in the fight. Did you notice he walks with a limp?"

"No."

"Well, he does. Took a bullet in the knee and another in the shoulder. The shoulder healed right, but the knee went stiff. Sort of like yours might do if you don't let Dog Woman keep adding them poultices."

"Why would Moss Taylor be ambushing people?"

"He hates the Utes. He's led men against us. He's bushwhacked our people. He'd kill us off like the wolves that raid his herds, if he could figure out a way to do it."

"And you think that maybe by ambushing Abe Long and . . ."

"Abe Long was one of the men ambushed?" Johnny asked.

"That's right. Did you know him?"

"I did. He was better'n all of 'em put together. He helped out the Utes once." Johnny's voice hardened. "Abe Long was another thorn in Moss Taylor's side. I'd say that it makes sense that he was one of the others ambushed."

Clint frowned. "I'll talk to old Moss Taylor. But, of course, he'll deny the fact that he's part of this puzzle. I'm going to need something I can pin facts onto."

"Not if you take me along when you go to visit Moss."

"Why's that?"

"Because," Johnny said matter-of-factly, "I'll stand in the trees, and when I get that old Indian-hatin' son of a bitch in my rifle sights, I'll put a hole through his heart big enough to run your fist through."

Clint shook his head. "It can't work that way."

"Why not?"

"Because," Clint said, talking to Midan as well as the old mountain man, "when I do discover who is really behind the killings, I'll need to bring him to justice. Only after we get his confession will the people of Butte City finally believe that the Utes had nothing to do with the killings."

Johnny didn't like the Gunsmith's reasoning, but he had to agree with it. "Fine," he said, "you let me hang Moss up by his thumbs and peel a few patches of skin off his hide with my dullest hunting knife and I guarantee we'll get him to make his confession."

"That wouldn't count."

"Well do you just expect that mean bastard to confess that he's the ambusher?"

"No," Clint replied, "I do not. But somehow, I need to find evidence against Moss Taylor—if he is the guilty party—and it has to be strong and convincing."

"How?" Midan asked bluntly.

"I don't know yet. But I tell you one thing, just hearing about him being at that fight and the fact that he hates the Ute people is reason to suspect that he is the man behind the full moon ambushings."

"I'd be willing to bet he's the one," Johnny said. "He blames the Utes for his bad knee. In that same fight, he lost his father and his older brother. He's always sworn to get even and wipe out Midan's people."

Clint nodded his head. The facts all fit neatly enough together to make him think that old Moss Taylor, long ago crippled and left without a father and a brother, was determined to turn Butte City against the Indians. After all, Moss had been the one stirring up the crowd the day that Clint and Sheriff

Denton had returned from the Rocking Horse Ranch gunfight.

"All right," Clint said, so absorbed by thought that he forgot about his own bad knee and turned to grab up his things as if to depart. The knee betrayed him, and he stifled a cry and almost fell. Both Johnny and Midan grabbed and supported him.

"Lie down," Johnny ordered. "Dog Woman will be comin' over here any minute to replace that poultice, and she'll be mad as hell anyway about you being on your feet."

Clint didn't argue. He allowed himself to be lowered back down to the buffalo robe. His knee was throbbing painfully. He felt sick and a little dizzy, so he closed his eyes and focused his mental powers as he went over what he had just learned about Moss Taylor.

Yes, it all fit, he thought, as Dog Woman appeared with another scalding poultice.

"Ouch!" he cried, sitting bolt upright. "Dammit, I . . ."

Dog Woman's head snapped up and her dark eyes blazed at the Gunsmith, but her hand held the fresh and steaming poultice tight against the Gunsmith's injured knee.

Sweat burst across Clint's forehead and he gasped, "How can you hold it there with your bare hands?"

The woman said nothing.

Johnny Irons's voice cut between them. "She's the Utes' most honored shaman. Used to be we had a medicine man, but he weren't any good. Dog Woman is damned good. She's half-Mexican, half-Apache.

Most of what she learned was with Geronimo's band. She doesn't feel pain herself. She can pick up a burning coal right out of the camp fire and drop it back without feelin' a damned thing."

"I find that hard to believe," Clint said, gazing into the medicine woman's blank eyes.

"Show him how you can pick up a piece of coal," Johnny said to the woman in Spanish.

Dog Woman turned and looked curiously at Johnny; then she reached over to the fire and grabbed a fiery stick and held it up before the Gunsmith's eyes. When he nodded, she pitched the burning stick back into the camp fire and no one even appeared to notice.

"See what I mean? She don't feel pain. Watch this."

Before Clint could object, Johnny reached out and pinched a hunk of Dog Woman's upper arm flesh between his thumb and forefinger. He pinched the flesh so hard he shivered with the effort. Dog Woman just stared at him.

"Stop it!" Clint ordered.

Johnny released the flesh. "See what I mean? She's got no feeling—good, or bad."

Clint was appalled. He had never seen someone who had no pain or pleasure sensations. He studied the girl for a moment. She was rather pretty in a coarse and somehow sensual way and probably in her early twenties. Clint could speak Spanish and so he said to her, "Show me your hand. The one that picked up that burning brand from the fire."

She raised her hand, her expression now curious. He examined her palm and it was as hard as bull hide. He touched the back of her hand and it was also very tough. Dog Woman seemed to have very thick skin, and she was quite hairy. She even had a trace of a mustache.

"Ain't she something, though?" Johnny said. "No man will have her, and even the Apaches thought she was possessed by the evil spirits. That's why they sold her to a fella who turned around and resold her to the Utes. By then, she'd been recognized as a medicine woman with special powers."

Clint lay back and nodded to Dog Woman that it was all right with the poultice. She studied him without any sign of interest, then indicated that he was to hold the poultice on himself while she went and soaked another in boiling water.

"Doesn't she ever speak?"

"Never heard her once. She understands Spanish, but she can't talk it. Midan says that her tongue was cut out. I don't know. When she eats, I've tried to look into her mouth, but she turns her head away and I can't tell if she's got a tongue or not."

"I see."

"You do as she says," Johnny warned. "Dog Woman isn't the kind to be messed around with."

"I can see that."

"There have been a few who tried."

"And what happened to them?" Clint asked, watching Dog Woman move away and seeing the nice shape of her slender hips under her buckskins.

"They paid for it."

"How?"

"She put a spell on 'em and they got sick. And then she wouldn't treat them with her medicines until they gave her payment. Dog Woman is pretty rich now and feared too."

Clint nodded. He saw Dog Woman meet an old Ute at the entrance of the wickiup, and it was the old man who deferred and let her have the right of way. That alone told the Gunsmith that the mysterious Dog Woman was indeed respected and very powerful.

THIRTEEN

In the days that followed, Clint often found cause to wonder about the Ute medicine woman who hovered over him constantly with her poultices and occasional chants and imprecations to her Indian spirits. Dog Woman seemed to display neither emotion nor feeling, but once when a puppy was kicked by an older Ute for entering the wickiup, Dog Woman flew into a rage. She scooped the yelping puppy up and her eyes blazed at the offending Indian, who shrank from her great displeasure.

Clint watched Dog Woman take the puppy and carefully examine its ribs and legs to see if any were broken. Satisfied that the pup was merely frightened and bruised, she cradled it in her arms and the puppy quit yelping.

"You have a kind heart," Clint said in his best Spanish and loud enough for Dog Woman's ears alone. She looked up and then she almost smiled as the puppy licked her face.

She does feel pleasure and pain, Clint thought to himself. She not only feels, but she watches and she observes everything. I think that she desperately wants to escape this camp and I also think that maybe her tongue isn't cut out at all and that she can really speak. I wonder what her real name is?

These thoughts and questions entered the Gunsmith's mind as powerfully but unbidden as strong March winds. He did not have any basis for them, but they formed and he was certain that he was right about the woman. Clint was also certain about something else and that was that Dog Woman had formed an attachment to him. Oh, it wasn't obvious, but sometimes he caught her staring at him when she thought he was not looking. At such moments, her face and eyes were no longer blank but filled with a softer expression. When he caught her at such unguarded moments, she would look away very suddenly, almost as if she were embarrassed.

"Dog Woman indicates to us that you're ready to move," Johnny Irons announced one afternoon. "She says that you're finally strong enough to sleep outdoors."

Clint knew that the weather had turned nice again, and he was more than ready to leave the smoky and fetid confines of the huge Ute wickiup. "That'd be fine."

"How long you think it will be before you're ready to go back to Butte City?"

Clint had been testing his injured knee every day. It wasn't able to fully support his weight, but it was healing nicely and it was clear that it had not been broken. "I could ride out tomorrow."

"You'll probably have to walk unless you want to trade something for an Indian pony."

"I want my six-gun and ammunition back," Clint said, expecting an argument.

Instead, Johnny nodded. "I never was no thief. I only took 'em because I thought you was a goner."

"Well, obviously, I'm not. So give them back."

"You got nothing else that these people would trade for a sound horse."

"Then I guess I'll just have to walk," Clint said, "unless you want to borrow a pony for me."

"Why the hell should I do a dumb thing like that? You already owe fifty dollars on the last horse you borrowed."

Clint had to admit that he was a mighty poor risk. "The sooner that I return to Butte City and get this ambushing thing sorted out and Moss Taylor in jail, the less likelihood there will be that the townsfolk will come storming up here looking to wipe out these Indian people."

Johnny opened his mouth to argue, but then snapped it shut because Clint's words made good sense. After toeing the earth for a few minutes with his moccasin, he grumbled, "Maybe we can find you some runty little pony that's strong enough to get you down to the valley before it dies."

"If you don't," Clint warned, "it'll be weeks before I can put this knee to the task of hiking out of these high mountains and all the way down to Butte City."

Johnny went away then, and Dog Woman came to indicate to Clint that she was ready to help him move outside. She assisted him to his feet and slipped her arm around his waist. He reached for his crutch, but she batted it away and shook her head.

"So," he said, "you want to be the one I lean on, huh?"

Dog Woman nodded and Clint leaned heavily on the slender half-breed girl, who hugged his waist and helped him out of the wickiup.

Once clear of his cramped confinement, Clint stopped and took a deep breath of the fragrant pines. "I should have moved out here in the open days ago," he said. "This high mountain air is a tonic."

Dog Woman looked up into his eyes and then she did smile. Before Clint could say anything, she helped him along until they entered a willow thicket and then came to rest on a grassy spot beside a stream. She stopped and indicated that this was the place where he was to rest until he was ready to return to the white village.

"Mighty nice spot," Clint said, sitting down and feeling the warm sun on his face. "Nice enough for a picnic."

Her expression told Clint that Dog Woman did not know the word "picnic."

"It just means a nice place to eat outdoors," he explained. "One that a man would share on a real nice day with a beautiful young woman like yourself."

Dog Woman blushed and hurried away through the willows. She reappeared a few minutes later with the buffalo robe he'd been using in the wickiup. She spread the heavy robe neatly beside the stream and turned to leave.

"Whoa," Clint said, grabbing her wrist and pulling her down beside him.

For an instant, Dog Woman's black eyes flashed and then the warning passed and her eyes closed. Clint took that as a sign that she wanted to be kissed and told that she was pretty.

"You're a beautiful woman," he said in Spanish. "A señorita with great heart and compassion. You saved my leg, I know that. Now, I'd like to repay you."

His hand smoothed the buckskin stretched taut across Dog Woman's breasts. They felt full beneath her buckskins, and he began to rub the buckskin back and forth to see if the woman really had no sensations of pain or pleasure. The experiment only lasted a few seconds, and then Dog Woman sighed with pleasure. She sat up quickly and Clint thought she was going to run away, but instead she yanked the buckskin dress up over her head, tossed it into the thickets, and smiled broadly.

"Wow!" he said with admiration as he gazed at her lush body. "You're quite a woman."

She leaned forward, cupping her own breasts. They were dusted with dark, short hair or fuzz. Hair or fuzz, it didn't bother Clint or detract from Dog Woman's sensuality. In fact, it might even have enhanced it.

The Gunsmith took Dog Woman's right breast in his mouth and tongued her nipple until it was as hard as licorice candy. He could hear her moan softly and he smiled. "There's nothing wrong with your ability to feel pleasure."

"No," she gasped in English as she fumbled for his belt buckle. "But like all white men, you talk too damn much!"

Clint was so surprised to hear Dog Woman speak that he tried to jerk his head back, but Dog Woman wasn't having any of that. She crushed his lips to her bosom even as her fingers tore open his pants and then found his already rising manhood.

"Easy on the bad knee," he warned.

"It's not the knee I'm after."

Clint quickly learned that Dog Woman was all business. She quickly had his pants pushed down around his knees and wasn't willing to let him waste the time it took even to remove his boots. Her thick, callused hands ought to have felt terrible on his already throbbing manhood, but they didn't. Dog Woman's hands had a power of their own and now, as she squatted down on him, they guided his rod into the center of her lush growth of pubic hair. He felt himself being sucked up into her body and then squeezed by her hot depths.

He looked up at the woman as he gripped her bouncing hips and said, "Dog Woman, do you want a long or a short ride?"

In reply, she toppled forward and began kissing him wildly. All the while, her body was thrusting powerfully at his hips, driving them into the buffalo robe. She began to moan and grunt. She broke into a sweat and when he finally rolled her over and mounted her like a stallion, Dog Woman locked her legs around the Gunsmith's waist and her eyes flashed with pleasure.

"Do it hard!" she ordered, grunting each time he plunged into her again. "Harder!"

Clint was still at a little less than full strength, but he did owe Dog Woman his best and so he gave her everything he had. He used her as fiercely as he'd ever used any woman, and yet the Gunsmith made sure that her pleasure kept building higher and higher. When she finally stiffened and her eyes rolled up into her forehead, Clint gave her one last hard thrust and his own seed began to spurt into Dog Woman as she quivered with ecstasy, her thighs shaking like the leaves on an aspen.

"Well," Clint said, rolling over and staring up through the limbs of the overhanging trees. "How was it?"

"Damned good! You do again soon, huh?"

He chuckled. "I'm sure planning on it. But if I'm supposed to leave this village and help the Utes, then I've got to save some of my strength for the long walk down to Butte City."

"You no walk. We ride my ponies."

Clint started with surprise. "What do you mean, *we* ride?"

"I go too."

"But you're the Utes' best shaman! Midan and the rest will never let you go."

"You help me. I helped you. We escape tonight."

"Now wait a minute," Clint said, suddenly very worried. "The last thing I need is for the Ute people to turn against me. I can't just run out on them in the night with their number one medicine healer."

Dog Woman frowned. "I go alone then."

Clint took a deep breath. This was all moving too fast. There were some things that needed to be understood. "Listen, Dog Woman, why do you want to go?"

"I have family."

"You do?"

"Mother and three sisters in Mexico. Apaches kill father and brothers. Take me as slave."

"How old were you then?"

"Seven." Dog Woman looked away suddenly, and Clint noticed how her dark eyes misted. "It very hard with Apaches. I almost die. Long time, want to die. Get very sick. Old woman teach me good Apache medicine. I learn best not to speak."

"Well, you had most of us fooled."

"Even Midan. He not know I speak."

"How do you pick up fiery coals and . . . and I saw Johnny pinch your skin. You didn't cry out or show any kind of pain."

"Apaches teach not to show pain." Dog Woman touched her forehead. "Think strong and no feel."

Clint knew that the Apaches were renowned for their ability to suffer extreme pain and deprivation. They could survive and even function for days longer than a white man when deprived of food or water. He had never before seen them pick up a burning ember without exhibiting pain or damage to the flesh, but Clint was sure that it was possible and Dog Woman's hands were like bull hide from some kind of labor that she must have endured while an Apache slave.

"I can't take you all the way to Mexico," he said. "I've got too many troubles of my own."

"You take away from here. I go to Mexico alone."

"And what if Midan refuses to let you go?"

"I kill him tonight."

All at once, Clint realized that Dog Woman was Midan's woman. He groaned. "I don't think that would be such a good plan. You see, if you killed Midan, the others would kill us. Then, what would have been accomplished?"

Dog Woman frowned and lowered her eyes. She seemed to consider this for several minutes and finally she said, "I buy freedom with ponies. Not to worry, Clint. Save two ponies."

The Gunsmith figured that Dog Woman's mind was made up and that she would do whatever it took to return to Mexico. The best and maybe the only thing that he could do was try to stay out of the trouble and let Dog Woman and Midan work this sudden separation out together and in peace.

"Good luck," he said. "And if you can get us out of here with two ponies, we can leave tomorrow. The sooner I get back to Butte City, the better."

Dog Woman nodded. Then, without even asking if the Gunsmith was ready, she rolled over onto her back, spread her shapely legs, and grabbed Clint by his slightly flaccid manhood.

"Hurry," she ordered. "I go speak to Midan soon."

Clint wasn't used to a woman jerking him around like that, but he figured he did owe Dog Woman his leg and maybe a whole lot more. So he allowed himself to be pulled as if on a dog's leash and then stuffed into Dog Woman's hairy little hole. When her hips began to rock back and forth, then around and around, Clint felt himself fill her to a bursting.

"All right," he wheezed as their bodies began to surge against each other, "after you tell Midan we're leaving, we both might be shot. Might as well enjoy ourselves as best we can."

In reply, Dog Woman yipped with pleasure.

That night was one of the longest that Clint could remember. About sunset, he and Dog Woman had coupled once more beside the stream and then she'd bathed, dressed, and gone back into the Ute village. He had half expected her to return or, in the very worst case, for Midan and his strongest young warriors to return and kill or even torture him. Fortunately, neither happened and the sleepless night passed without incident.

But just after dawn, Dog Woman appeared. She looked haggard and worn. Her lips were puffy, but she was leading two good saddled ponies. When the Gunsmith tried to ask her what had happened in the village and how Midan had reacted to her decision to leave and return to Mexico, Dog Woman just pursed her lips and shook her head to indicate that she did not want to talk.

"So," Johnny said, as Clint hopped from a rock into the saddle and gingerly tested his game knee, "you're takin' the best little medicine woman we got and runnin' south."

"I'm not *running* anywhere," Clint said. "I'm heading back to Butte City. Dog Woman is determined to return to her people in Mexico."

"And she just happens to make that decision when you're humpin' her?"

Clint sighed. He wanted to just ride away; he was in no mood for a confrontation. But Johnny Irons's attitude needed an adjustment. "Yeah," he said, "I humped her, but she's wanted to leave for a long time. She's tired of being the Ute village slave."

"She's lived well among these people."

"Ha!" Dog Woman's lips curled. "Johnny Irons, you lie!"

He took an involuntary step backward with surprise. "So, it's true. You was able to speak all the time and you was just fakin'."

"My name is Rosita Lopez, and I am from the state of Chihuahua. I belong to a small village."

"Rosita," Clint said. "That's a pretty name. It fits."

"Hell," Johnny snarled, "Rosita or Dog Woman, it don't matter. Same person. And either way, they won't even remember you back in Mexico."

Johnny scratched himself, then added, "Dog Woman, you've been with our people for what? Eight years now? Our people have taken care of you. Fed and clothed you and . . ."

"They are not my people and they are not *your* people, old man!" she said harshly. "You forget your white man's blood!"

If Johnny had it in mind to lecture the girl, all that changed with those devastating words. Clint watched as the man actually seemed to shrink a little in his buckskins. And then, he drew Clint's six-gun from his belt and handed it up to him on the pony. No mention was made of the box of ammunition, and Clint didn't want to push his luck.

"I'll see you again," he said. "I'll get Moss Taylor, if he's the one behind those ambushes."

"Yeah," Johnny said. "And I'll give you until the next new moon to do 'er. After that, I'll bushwhack him myself."

Clint started to argue that bushwhacking Moss Taylor was the very worst thing that Johnny could do. But before the argument could form on his lips, the old man pivoted around and was gone.

The Gunsmith didn't see Midan or any of the other Utes. They probably had already learned that Dog Woman had traded all but two of her prized ponies for their freedom.

"Come on," Clint said to the Ute pony. "We got a long ride before this day is over."

He overtook Rosita, and they rode swiftly down the mountains. At noon, they stopped to rest and let the horses graze for an hour, then they remounted and rode on. In the late afternoon they passed the twin peaks where Johnny Irons's cabin lay hidden at the base of a landslide, just overlooking a clear alpine lake. Clint said nothing of this, and Rosita did not seem inclined to conversation.

He openly studied her pretty face, trying to guess what her thoughts might be, but the Apache in her blood made her as inscrutable as the face of a carved and painted puppet. Clint wondered if she would want to spend any time among the white people of Butte City.

Probably not. Clint had a strong feeling that Dog Woman... or rather, Señorita Rosita Lopez, was about to pass out of his life as mysteriously as she had entered.

FOURTEEN

Clint had guessed right about Rosita Lopez. The moment that Butte City was in view, she pulled her horse up and would go no nearer to the town.

"You need some food and rest," Clint argued.

But Rosita just shook her pretty head. "Not in a white man's town."

Clint looked at the old single-shot rifle that Rosita carried along with a battered Army Colt that had not yet been converted to rimfire cartridges. "I sure wish that you would come on into town. I could get my tools and at least go over those weapons of yours. You might just need them before you reach your home village in Mexico."

"They shoot straight, and my village is near the border."

"But you don't even have a rain slicker! No bedroll or anything."

She looked at him with a little sadness. "Why don't you come to my village of Janos, Mexico? We could be happy there."

He smiled and realized that he found the idea quite appealing. "You tempt me, girl. You really do.

But I've a job to do here and it can't wait any longer. Maybe if you stayed awhile then . . ."

"I also cannot wait any longer," she said softly.

Clint dismounted. "This is your pony. You take him."

"No."

"Take him or I'll turn him loose. You've a long, long road to travel and you can use an extra horse."

Rosita finally nodded. "You can walk that far?"

"Oh, sure."

"Good-bye, señor."

"Good-bye."

Clint watched her gallop away and begin to circle Butte City. He had to curb a strong impulse to call her back. He still could. And she'd come.

"*Vaya con Dios*," he whispered, pulling his Stetson low and trudging on toward town.

His return went unheralded. When he arrived at Thelma's bedside she looked so thrilled to see him that his thoughts of Rosita Lopez vanished like mist in sunlight.

"What happened to you?" she cried, hugging him tightly.

"I had a little accident in the mountains. A horse went over the side of a gorge and we tumbled a ways."

"You're lucky that you weren't killed!"

"I've always been lucky," Clint said, briefly describing his ordeal with Johnny Irons, Midan, and the Ute people but deciding to leave out the story of his attraction to the wild and independent Rosita.

"We'd better have Dr. Potter check you over."

"I'm fine."

Thelma went over to her door and closed, then locked it. "Then I'll check you over."

Clint didn't have the heart to tell the woman that he was completely spent. And yet, his face must have revealed his lack of enthusiasm because Thelma stopped short and said, "You really are not feeling well. I can see that now. You're going to bed, Clint, but you're going to have to do it alone for the time being."

He almost sighed with relief. The half mile walk from where he'd said good-bye to Rosita to this boardinghouse room had set his knee to throbbing and it felt swelled up a little.

"I could sure use a bath," he said, as she unbuttoned his shirt.

Thelma wrinkled her nose. "I should say that you could! Why, you smell like you've been rolling around with . . . I don't know. A bear or a dog."

"Not quite," he said with a straight face.

Thelma unlocked the door, stuck her head out, and called, "Hey, Ching Lee! Would you bring hot water for a bathee!"

"Bathee?"

"That's Chinese talk for bath," Thelma explained, as she pushed Clint down on the bed and began to wrench off his boots. "I think he appreciates my extra effort to speak a little Chinese."

"I'm sure that he does," Clint deadpanned.

"Whew!" Thelma said. "You really do smell rank. And this knee is all puffed up. I'll get the doctor right away."

"The knee is going to be fine," Clint told her. "And you can get the doctor later. After I've soaked in a bath for about an hour and had a glass of whiskey and a chance to recover."

"Fine," Thelma said. "How are you? When you didn't return from going to find Johnny Irons, I was so afraid that you were shot up there. That crazy old coot isn't to be trusted."

"He tried to shoot me, all right. But after I gave him a little introduction, we came to an understanding."

"Did he take you to Midan?"

"Yes," Clint said, and then he told Thelma about his trip up to the Ute camp and his encounter with the Ute chief. Later, after Ching Lee had finished filling the bathtub and had left for the last time, Clint ended up saying, "And so, I have a hunch that Moss Taylor is the most likely fella behind all these ambushings."

Thelma's brow wrinkled. "But why would he do them just during the time of the full moon?"

"So people would jump to some ridiculous conclusion that the ambushings *had* to be due to Ute revenge."

"I see," Thelma said, not sounding like she was very convinced. "But how are you going to prove any of this?"

"I have no idea. What I figure to do is ride out tomorrow and confront the man."

"At his ranch? With all his men standing around?" Thelma looked appalled by the idea. "Are you trying to get yourself killed?"

"No," Clint said, "but I don't know how else to go about getting to the bottom of these ambushings."

"There must be a better way," Thelma said. "Either you'll get riddled by Moss's crowd of gunfighters and hard cases, or else he'll just flatly deny having anything to do with the ambushings. Either way, you lose."

Clint had the sinking feeling that Thelma was probably right. He closed his eyes and allowed himself to sink deeper into the hot, soapy water. It felt wonderful.

"Your knee looks awful."

"You should have seen it before the Ute medicine woman..."

"Woman?"

"Yeah," Clint said, instantly realizing his mistake. "Sometimes they're women."

"Young women?" Thelma asked suspiciously.

"Naw."

Fortunately, Thelma decided not to pursue the matter. "Sit forward and let me scrub your back."

Clint rolled his head to and fro against the tin tub, barely able to keep his eyes open. "Leave my back alone, Thelma. If you want to do something, get me a glass of good whiskey. That's all I'll need to be content."

Thelma dutifully returned with the whiskey and when Clint had tossed it down, he closed his eyes and sighed, "I feel like I've died and gone to heaven."

"Not yet you haven't," Thelma said, undressing and crawling into the tub. "Not until we've had each other you haven't."

Clint wanted to protest, he really did. At least, for the first few moments.

They were awakened by a loud hammering on Thelma's door. "Adams! Adams, are you in there?"

Thelma bounded out of bed. "It's the sheriff."

"Tell him I'll come around tomorrow morning."

Thelma went to the door, unlocked it, and opened it a crack. "Clint says to tell you that . . ."

Denton threw his shoulder to the door and knocked Thelma aside.

"Hey!" she cried.

Clint always kept his six-gun close, but this time it was not close enough, and the sheriff cocked his gun and aimed it right at Clint's face before he could arm himself.

"Touch that gun and you're a dead man," Denton warned.

"What the hell is wrong with you?" Clint demanded.

"You're under arrest for murder."

"Murder!" Clint was stark naked, but he didn't care a whit as he bounded out of Thelma's bed. "Murder of who?"

"John Lincoln."

"The gambler?"

"That's right. You took his horse and when you didn't come back, he went out to find you. We just found him ambushed about ten miles north of town."

"Well, I sure as hell didn't do it!"

"Yeah you did," Denton said. "There was a witness."

"Who?"

Denton smiled maliciously. "As a matter of fact, the murder occurred on Moss Taylor's ranch and he saw you."

Clint sputtered, "That's impossible! I was coming down the mountain from up by those twin peaks. I'd gone to see Johnny Irons and the Ute people. Why, from what I've heard, Moss Taylor's ranch isn't anywhere near along the path I rode."

"Sorry," Denton said, making it clear that he was anything but sorry. "Mr. Taylor said he saw you ride up and take cover. While he was trying to figure out what for, along came Lincoln and you shot him with your rifle. Drilled him through the heart with one hell of a fine shot."

Thelma threw herself at Denton and cried, "Shoot him, Clint!" But Denton must have expected Thelma to act because he set his feet and pistol-whipped her across the crown of her head, and she dropped to the floor. Clint didn't have a chance to grab his weapon.

"Go ahead," Denton pleaded. "I think you not only shot that gambler so you didn't have to tell him you'd lost his damned horse up in those mountains, but you also are the one that is behind all these ambushings."

"That's crazy!"

"Is it?" Denton leered. "Not so crazy. I haven't figured out your motive yet, but I suspect that I eventually will. Most likely, you were hired by someone to carry out those ambushes and frighten the town. I think you were probably hired by a damned land speculator."

"Land speculator? What the hell are you talking about now?"

"I think a land speculator hired you to scare Butte City into a ghost town so's he could buy it up cheap. After that, you'd move on and the ghost would be laid to rest. The land speculator would own all the town property and be able to sell it back and reap a fortune."

"You're as crazy as a coot."

"Like a fox, you mean," Denton crowed. "I figured your game out, and when Mr. Taylor testifies to the circuit judge what he seen you do, you'll be winging your way to hell for all the killing you've done in your lifetime."

Clint could see that it was pointless to argue with this lunatic. The man was so excited and enraged he might even pull the trigger. Clint knelt beside Thelma and examined the knot on her head. "You'll pay for this, Denton."

"If she hadn't tried to fight me, I wouldn't have had to put that knot on her damned head."

"You hit her harder than was necessary," Clint said with an edge to his voice. "You could have just knocked her to the floor instead of using the butt of that pistol to open her scalp. She's going to need Doc Potter."

"After I've got you behind bars, I'll get ahold of the doc. Now, put your hands over your head and..."

"I'm going to get dressed first," Clint said. "I'll be damned if I'll be marched down the hall and across the street wearing nothing but goose pimples."

Denton chuckled a little obscenely. "I guess I probably had better let you put on your boots and clothes. Might be some respectable ladies out there would see what you been usin' on Thelma."

The sheriff smiled even wider and braved a quick glance down at the unconscious woman. "By the way, Adams, how is Thelma in the hay?"

Clint had to control himself from rushing at Denton with the express intent of breaking his neck. "You're a disgrace to the law profession."

Denton flushed. "Oh yeah? Well, I may not be the best there ever was, but neither was you, Gunsmith. You couldn't hold a candle to Wyatt Earp and Hickok!"

Clint reached for his clothes, thinking that he might be able to hurl them into Denton's gun and deflect his aim just long enough to reach and disable the man. But Denton was wary and backed to the door. "You try anything at all, you're a dead man," he warned.

The Gunsmith dressed quickly and was herded out the door and across the street. Moss Taylor was waiting by the sheriff's office, smoking a big cigar.

"Nice work, Sheriff."

"Hell, he wasn't so tough. Surrendered without a fight."

Clint glared at the old rancher. "Did you really tell this idiot that you saw me ambush that gambler?"

"That's right."

"You're a liar."

Taylor's face flushed and he cocked back his fist and swung at Clint, but the Gunsmith ducked and pounded a heavy uppercut to the rancher's solar plexus. The old man's mouth flew open and he gasped for air like a sucker fish tossed on the beach. He turned fish-belly white too. When he tried to claw for his gun, Clint smashed the old bastard behind the ear, and that's when Denton's gun barrel did the same thing to Clint.

He went to his knees, and then Denton hit him again and that was all that the Gunsmith remembered.

FIFTEEN

"How's Thelma feeling?" Clint asked as soon as Dr. Potter reached his jail cell.

"She's woozy, but I don't think that she has a concussion." Potter looked at Clint through the bars. "How are you?"

"I'm damned upset," Clint gritted, keeping his voice low so that Denton could not overhear this conversation.

"Turn around and let me look at the back of your scalp."

Clint obliged the doctor. "Ouch!"

"You've got as nasty a laceration as Thelma. The sheriff showed no favoritism when he pistol-whipped the both of you."

"I'll heal," Clint said. "Doc, have you heard what they're charging me with?"

"Sure I have." The doctor scowled. "Everyone in town is talking about your arrest. You've been charged with ambushing John Lincoln as well as being behind the other killings that have kept Butte City up in arms."

"That's right. And Moss Taylor is going to commit

perjury in an effort to see me hang."

The doc heaved a deep sigh. "You're up against a stacked deck, Clint. Moss Taylor is the most powerful man in this county and he owns both the sheriff and Judge Banes."

"Who is he?"

"He's the judge who will hold a kangaroo court and sentence you to death tomorrow."

Clint's jaw dropped. "Tomorrow?" he managed to whisper.

"That's right."

"But I thought that he was a circuit judge and . . ."

"He is a circuit judge, although I'd be more inclined to call him a *circus* judge because his court has nothing to do with justice."

"Yes, but . . ."

"As soon as you were arrested and brought here, Moss Taylor sent a coach out to find and return the judge. He's got an armed escort and it won't matter if Judge Banes is drunk, sober, or right in the middle of a trial. He'll be here tomorrow morning no matter what his condition."

"I see," Clint said quietly. "I'm beginning to feel that they really want to get this trial over with in a hurry and get me out of their way—permanently."

"Sure. Clint, I don't know why the big hurry, but you can bet your trial won't last the morning and they might even try and have you swing before tomorrow at sundown."

This was hard news for the Gunsmith. Devastating news, in fact. He'd thought that, with enough time, he might be able to figure out some decent defense to discredit Moss Taylor's perjurious testimony. And even though he had no money to hire a lawyer, liveryman Bud York had assured Clint only minutes earlier that he had friends who would take up a collection for a legal defense. Now, all those plans seemed to be in imminent danger of being swept away by this conspiracy to see him hang by tomorrow.

"Look, Clint, I have some money and I'll gladly give it to you for a lawyer, but there isn't anyone in town that would represent you. There's only one lawyer in Butte City and I'm afraid that he . . ."

"Don't say it," Clint interrupted. "That lawyer owes his livelihood to Moss Taylor."

"Yes. But he isn't worth a damn anyway, and he'd be easy enough to beat if we had some time. The trouble is, Moss Taylor's testimony that he actually saw you kill Lincoln is going to be almost impossible to overcome unless you have some kind of proof that you were elsewhere."

Clint squeezed the jail bars until his knuckles grew white. "I'm running out of time. Seems to me, the only reason that Moss Taylor and his crowd are trying to railroad this trial through so fast and get me hanged is that they know I'm innocent and that my conviction and hanging will sweep all this ambushing business under the rug."

"But it'll come right back to haunt them the first time that someone is ambushed by a full moon."

"Yeah," Clint said, "but I'll be in the grave by then and it won't matter as far as saving my ass."

Doc Potter nodded morosely. "Thelma says you've

got a bad knee. I thought I'd take a look."

"Not much point," Clint said. "Not if I'm bound to hang tomorrow."

"I'd like to see it anyway." The doctor turned around and glared at Sheriff Denton. "This man has an injured left knee. I need to treat it."

Denton had been trying to overhear the conversation while pretending to read a week-old newspaper. "To hell with that, Doc! He's probably going to hang tomorrow anyway. And he's broke, so he can't pay you for your services."

"I have a Hippocratic oath to fulfill. I insist on treating this man regardless of his fate."

The sheriff laid down his paper and shook his head. "I don't think so, Doc."

Potter blushed with anger. "Fine," he snapped, "but there will come a day when you're going to be sick or injured or shot. And when that day comes, Sheriff Denton, you had damn sure better hope that your friends can get you to the next town because I'll refuse to treat you!"

Denton came to his feet. He must have realized that the doctor was serious and the threat was too.

"Now, Doc," he said, forcing a grin, "there ain't no need to get all huffy and upset. This here man is a murderer. I'm the town sheriff. It ain't anywhere near the same."

"It is to me," the doctor said firmly. "I have an oath to uphold, and if you cause me to break it, then I'll break it once more just when you are in great need of my services."

"You'd let me suffer and die?"

"I would."

Denton expelled a deep breath. "All right," he allowed, "but I'm going to need to search you and your medical kit for a weapon. That's standard procedure."

"Then, Sheriff, commit the insult at once and let me treat my patient."

While Clint stood back and watched, the sheriff conducted a very quick and ineffective search. He looked embarrassed, and the doctor's threat was clearly on his mind when he said apologetically, "All right, you can go in there but only for a few minutes."

The doctor nodded. Denton drew his six-gun and pointed it at Clint. "All the way against the back wall."

Clint did as he was ordered. He waited as the cell door was opened and the doctor allowed to enter. The door was quickly relocked.

"Drop your pants and let me look at that knee," the doctor ordered.

Clint unbuckled his belt and dropped his pants. The doctor bent and studied the knee. "You've had a very bad accident. It's a wonder that this knee bends at all."

"Is it going to heal?"

"It will, if you have time. I think that the knee was probably dislocated and perhaps some interior tendons and ligaments torn. Let me see you bend it."

Clint bent the knee. It was swollen again but not too badly and there was little pain. "Can you do anything for it?"

"Not much," the doctor said, and without looking up, he slipped a two-shot derringer into Clint's left boot top. "Thelma sends her love and assistance."

"Thelma's help is very much appreciated," Clint said, pulling up his pants and feeling the mean little derringer slip down almost to his ankles.

The doctor stood up. "You're going to hang unless you can clear yourself or there is a sudden intervention."

"What the hell does *that* mean?" Denton demanded.

The doctor said, "Prayer creates miracles."

The sheriff relaxed. "Yeah, sure. Come on, Doc. Let's get you out of there."

When the doctor was outside and the jail door relocked, the sheriff relaxed and said, "Were I you, Gunsmith, I'd say my prayers, because you're going to be meeting Saint Peter before very damn long."

The doctor stuck his hand through the bars and shook with Clint. "Thelma sends her love as well as her prayers and assistance. She wanted to come with me, but I couldn't allow that. She's not well enough to stand up much, let alone undergo the strain of seeing you so miserably treated."

"Tell her that she's already done more than enough for me," Clint said, meaning every word of it.

"I just wish that you had a witness that could testify that you were nowhere near Moss Taylor's ranch when that gambler was ambushed," the doctor said. "Someone that would be so believable that even Judge Banes would have to declare a mistrial and set you free."

Clint almost blurted that he did have a witness—Rosita Lopez. But something made him realize that having the sheriff overhear this admission would be a critical mistake on his behalf.

"Yeah," he said, deciding right then that he would try and bust free of this cell and then find Rosita. If he could somehow talk her into returning to Butte City and testifying that he could not have been near Moss Taylor's ranch at the time that Lincoln was ambushed, the judge would have no choice but to free Clint.

The Gunsmith waited until late that evening. By then, he'd had a long nap and felt rested and ready for an all-night ride that might not end until he reached Janos, Mexico, wherever that might be located.

"Lights out," Sheriff Denton said, getting up from his desk chair and stretching.

Clint had already figured out that Denton intended to spend the night guarding him. The man had unfolded a small cot and rustled up some woolen blankets. Then, he'd spent the remainder of the evening sipping brandy and reading old newspapers.

"So," Clint said, "you're going to keep me company."

"Thought it was the right thing to do," Denton said. "A man ought not be alone during his last night on earth. But then, he really ought to have a woman like Thelma."

Clint knew that the sheriff wanted to goad him to anger, and he cut off the man by saying, "Thelma and I will spend a few more nights together before all this is said and done."

"Oh, I'd not be counting on that. I just heard that Judge Banes is down in Lander and he's being brought up tonight. He should be ready to hold court at nine o'clock tomorrow morning, drunk or sober."

"I thought a man was supposed to be represented by a lawyer and have the right to a fair trail."

"Not in this county." Denton chuckled. "Think of it this way, mister. You've lived a long time and you've killed a lot of men. But this time, your luck just ran out."

"Luck had damn little to do with it," Clint said. "The men I killed always needed killing. I think *you* need killing, Sheriff."

Denton's grin slipped badly. "Well, now!" he crowed, marching over to the cell and putting his hands on his hips. "I guess I might as well tell you that what you think don't mean nothing. You're already the same as a dead man."

"And so are you," Clint said, drawing the derringer out and aiming it at Denton's heart. "Open this cell."

Denton's eyes bugged. "Why . . . Doc Potter must have passed that to you!"

"Nope. I always carry a hide-out gun and you just didn't check me out close enough. Now open this door."

"I won't do it!"

"You will if you want to live," Clint said, cocking back the hammer to the derringer. "I have nothing to lose. I'll kill you where you stand."

"You shoot and people will come running."

"I don't think so," Clint said. "The walls to this

jail are thick and there's a lot of noise coming from the saloon just up the street. At any rate, that's a chance I'll just have to take."

Denton wavered. Clint could see how badly the lawman wanted to risk drawing his own gun and trying to save a bad situation. But he was facing real long odds and he must have realized that because he said, "My keys are in the desk drawer."

"No they're not. I saw you slip them into your vest. Quit stalling and open the damned door!"

Denton swore and found his keys. Eyes radiating hatred, he unlocked the jail cell door and then he kicked it open with his boot. "You'll never get away with this."

"Sure I will," Clint said. "Step inside."

When Denton stepped into the cell, Clint drew the man's Colt from his holster. "Have you ever had trouble sleeping at night, Sheriff?"

"Huh?"

"Sleeping. Do you have trouble going to sleep?"

"Well, I . . ."

"Not tonight you won't," Clint said, pistol-whipping the man very hard across his forehead.

Denton dropped face first to the rock floor and didn't move. Clint knew that the corrupt lawman would be out cold at least until morning. By then, the Gunsmith hoped to be well on his way south. Mexico was a long, long way and he wasn't at all sure if Rosita would consent to coming back to Butte City. She hated the white man's towns and it would take a lot of courage and incentive for her to do such a thing. She'd probably ask Clint to stay with her in

Mexico where his past would not matter and where the law would never find him.

But Clint wanted vindication and to clear his name. He wanted one other thing, and that was to make Moss Taylor appear a liar and then bring the man to justice for his crimes of murder, the latest being John Lincoln. And somewhere during all that, Clint meant to get down to his motive for the rash of moonlight murders.

SIXTEEN

Thelma had wanted to flee Butte City until the Gunsmith had been forced to admit to her that his only witness was a fiery young half-breed girl named Rosita Lopez who was riding hard for a little village in Mexico.

"Then I'll stay here," she said, sounding a little hurt and even betrayed. "You find this Mexican/Indian girl and bring her back to testify. I'll be waiting."

"I'll need a horse. I could just steal one, but...."

"No," Thelma said firmly. "I've already taken care of that. Bud York tells me that your own horse, Duke, is sound again."

"He is!" This was wonderful news to the Gunsmith.

"Yes. Bud has Duke saddled and waiting for you at his livery. Just be careful!"

"I will."

Clint kissed Thelma good-bye, and when he reached the door she called, "Clint?"

"Yes?"

AMBUSH MOON

"Is this Ute medicine woman beautiful?"

He frowned. "I wouldn't exactly say so."

"But she's younger than I am with a fine body and pretty face. Isn't that true?"

Clint knew better than to lie about it. "Yeah," he admitted. "She's young and pretty."

"And you also made love to her, didn't you?"

"Now what makes you think that?"

"Because," Thelma said, "you fled the Ute village together. That means that she must have trusted you greatly and wanted to be with you. Be honest with me, Clint."

"All right," he said, feeling a rush of guilt. "We did make love."

Thelma sighed. "I knew it. You're just too wild and handsome to be true to any one woman."

Clint started to protest, but Thelma said, "I've been resting in bed all day thinking about us and everything that's happened since we met."

"Now, Thelma," Clint cautioned, "sometimes it's best not to think too much. Especially when we've both just been pistol-whipped."

"That hasn't hurt my thinking. I've decided that I'd be foolish to count on you coming back to Butte City and then us getting married."

"Married?"

Clint's astonishment must have shown because Thelma said, "I can tell by your face that the idea of marriage scares you half to death."

"It's just that I never gave much thought to it," Clint stammered.

"And I doubt that you ever will."

Clint didn't have a ready answer for that, so he just stood beside the door for a minute.

"Thelma," he finally said, "by slipping me that derringer through Doc Potter, you saved my life. I owe you most anything—even marriage."

She sniffled and lifted her chin. "No thanks. That's not the way that a man is supposed to go into a marriage, and it's certainly not the way I'd want to get married. I mean, you don't do it out of debt or a sense of obligation."

Clint started to come back to Thelma. "It wouldn't exactly be an obligation."

"Stop! Not another step forward. You just turn around and march yourself to the livery and catch that girl. And once you do, if you're smart, you'll make love to her again and . . ."

"Thelma, stop it!"

" . . . and then you'll keep riding and not stop until you get to her village where you'll live happily ever after. Like people do in fairy tales."

"I wouldn't be happy in some sleepy Mexican village."

"Well, maybe not," Thelma conceded, "but you couldn't make me happy in a marriage born of obligation. We'd both be miserable after a year or two. And so, when you get to that livery, would you ask Mr. York if he'd come calling?"

"Bud?"

"Yes, Bud!"

"Why sure!" Clint went back to the door in a daze. "He'll be very happy to call on you, Thelma. When would you like him to stop by?"

Thelma sniffled and reached for a mirror and some powder for her face that was resting on a nightstand. "Tell him . . . tell him he can come by in about fifteen minutes."

Clint almost laughed outright. He should have realized that Thelma, while she really loved him, was not the kind of wither away or crawl into a hole and suffer a romantic rejection. Rather, she would have Bud York drooling and most likely in her bed before midnight. And the very best thing was, they were meant for each other. Bud was a wonderful man who'd secretly loved Thelma for years.

"Good-bye, Thelma."

"Good-bye," she said, fluffing up her hair and then dabbing powder on her nose. "And Clint?"

"Yes?"

"Be smart. Don't come back to Butte City and buck the long odds. This isn't your fight, and you've no reason to go up against Moss Taylor."

"That's where you're wrong," Clint replied. "He lied about me, and he's after this town for some reason. I'll not rest until I have the answers to some very puzzling questions."

Clint hurried unseen to the livery. Just as promised, Bud York had a fine saddle horse ready and waiting.

"I may get into trouble and not bring him back," Clint admitted to the man.

"That's all right. I think you ought to just keep riding and not look back."

"Thanks." Clint climbed stiffly into the saddle because of his hurt knee. "By the way, Bud, Thelma asked if you could come by for a visit."

"Thelma asked for me?"

"Yep."

Bud's eyes lit up. "Well, I thought that you and her were . . . well, you know."

"Not anymore."

Bud gulped. "When can I go see her?"

"She's waiting for you right now."

"Tonight!" The liveryman blushed, and his feet began to dance without his conscious bidding. "You mean, right now?"

"That's exactly what I mean."

"Wow!" The liveryman started to turn and dash out the door into the street.

"And Bud?" Clint called.

The man skidded to a halt beside the doorway. "Yeah?"

"If I were you, I'd take a bath first. If you own a razor, then shave. And put on some clean clothes. Yours are ripped and stiff with horseshit."

His eyes dropped to his shirt and his stiffly caked pants. "I guess I do sorta look rough, huh?"

"Yeah. Sorta. You see, Thelma is kind of special, and she likes a man to be clean and smell nice."

"I got some perfume water that a whore gave me once."

"Take the bath and shave, then put on some of that whore's cologne. Not too much, though. Just wet your palms and rub it . . . well, rub it wherever you happen to think best. Thelma will like it."

Protest formed in Bud's eyes. "But all that'd take me ten or fifteen minutes!"

"She'll be glad you took the time," Clint said. "Trust

AMBUSH MOON

me, Thelma will be real glad."

Bud eyed the door. It was clear that it was all he could do not to burst away in a sprint and race to Thelma's bedside.

"Are you sure?"

"I'm sure. You've been good to me and good to Duke. It's the least I can do to tell you the truth about that woman."

Bud nodded rapidly. "Well, you'd know. I mean, you're a ladies' man and I'm sort of a slob. Always have been and always will be. It comes with my profession."

"I disagree. You can operate this stable, get dirty in the day, and still take a bath every evening and shave every morning. And if you play your cards right, Thelma will fall in love and marry you."

Bud actually clasped his dirty hands together and Clint thought the man was going to swoon before he said, "There's no time for a hot bath so's I'm just going to jump into the horses' water trough with a bar of lye soap and a razor."

"That'll be fine. Just remember to drain the trough and rise it out so your horses don't drink the lye and get sick."

"I will!"

Clint tipped his hat and rode Duke out into the dark night. Being back on his own fine gelding made him feel good again. Really good. Duke was an extraordinarily fast and sound animal that could cover a lot of ground in a hell of a big hurry.

On Duke, the Gunsmith was dead sure that he could overtake Rosita long before she could reach Old Mexico.

SEVENTEEN

Less than twenty-five miles south of Butte City, Rosita Lopez had run into some extraordinarily bad luck. She had found what seemed to be an abandoned cabin with a corral to contain her weary Ute ponies while she slept for a few hours. Unfortunately, the cabin turned out to be a line shack, and Rosita had no sooner gotten to bed when a trio of drifting cattle rustlers had arrived.

"Holy Moses!" one of the rustlers shouted. "I tell you, our prayers have been answered. We found us a young and pretty woman!"

Rosita had tried to shoot them with her old Army cap and ball pistol, but one of the men doubled up his fist and smashed her in the jaw. Rosita wished that the blow had broken her neck because it would have been easier to die than endure what they quickly began to do to her after that.

And now, as she lay tied spread-eagled on the bunk waiting for the next man to have his pleasure, Rosita tried to find a calm place deep inside of her so that she could endure this outrage and survive long

AMBUSH MOON

enough to kill all three men and feed their bodies to the buzzards.

"How you doin', Rosita?" one of the cattle rustlers said as the trio sat around a crude table and played poker in their long underwear. "You ready for me again?"

"I kill you soon!" Rosita choked.

"Ha!" The man laughed. "I do like a woman with fire! And you got that, honey. I tell you, there will be no cattle rustlin' in this part of the country as long as we got you to keep the three of us busy."

Rosita struggled against her bonds, causing the three men to laugh all the louder.

"Hang on a little longer!" one of the other men called. "I can see that you're squirmin' with desire!"

More sick laughter. Rosita choked back tears of rage and outrage. What would happen to her when they finally grew weary of using her? Would they kill her? Probably, because they would be too ashamed to admit what animals they were and how it had taken all three of them to subdue and tie her to this bed.

Rosita expected torture first. There was a marrow-deep meanness about these three, and when they mounted her, they not only sought their pleasure, but also to inflict pain. They pinched and nipped her body and tried to make her beg for mercy. So far, she had held out against their cruelty, but Rosita was not sure how much longer she could remain strong.

There seemed to be no possibility of escape. Rosita's wrists and ankles were tied to the four bedposts, and, she was constantly watched. Not an hour went by that one of the bastards did not use her for his pleasure and then check the tightness of her bonds.

This is far worse than any quick death, she thought, this is worse than getting your neck broken or a bullet in your heart. What time was it anyway? These men did not sleep like normal people. They drank and gambled at night and took turns napping and raping her day and night.

Rosita was filled with despair for what might have been. Since she met Clint Adams, she had thought that she had at last found a man that she could love. But he had deserted her, and then she had pinned her hopes and chance for happiness on a village in Mexico that she could barely remember.

Were her mother and brothers still alive or had they been slaughtered by the Apaches? Did the fields grow tall with corn, or had the Apaches or the *federales* stolen the harvest and left her people to starve? Down in Mexico, one never knew what each year would bring. Maybe life and maybe death but most certainly heartache. Life with Midan and the Utes had been little better. Being a half-breed, she had earned respect through her medicine, but never love. Men wanted her, but always for their pleasure.

Like these animals.

"Hang on, Rosie!" one of the men called. "I'm getting the urge and I'm comin' to you as soon as I can win this hand."

Rosita stifled a sob deep in her throat. It would have been much better if they had shot her.

When Clint saw the line shack and Rosita's familiar Ute ponies, he was more than a little relieved and surprised. But when he saw the three other corralled horses and the light shining through the single grimy window, despite it being long after midnight, he became wary.

The Gunsmith knew how much Rosita disliked and mistrusted strangers. He knew how three unprincipled men might take advantage of her for their pleasure. In fact, as Clint tied Duke up in some thickets about a hundred yards from the cabin and drew his six-gun, he had a very bad feeling about what was going on inside the cabin.

He could hear raucous laughter, and as he drew nearer, it was obvious that a card game was in progress. Limping a little because of his sore knee, he slipped up to the cabin window. Removing his hat, he raised his head and tried to peer inside, but the window hadn't been washed in so long that it was covered with grime and dirt.

Clint crouched beside the cabin, trying to decide how best he might make his entrance. There was, after all, the possibility that the men inside had not harmed Rosita and were merely enjoying an all-night game of poker. If that were the case, what was Rosita doing?

Clint was still pondering this question when he heard one of the men hoot and yell, "Three of a kind!

I win another damned hand, and I claim the prize! Rosie, start twitchin' because I'm comin' over for a hard ride!"

"Lucky bastard," another voice spat. "It was my turn this time."

Clint had heard enough. A cold fury swept over him as he moved to the door of the cabin. Rearing back despite his bad knee, Clint kicked the door open with a bang.

The winner of the poker game was about to mount Rosie and when his head jerked around to see Clint, his jaw dropped open as his companions lunged for their six-guns. Clint shot the man poised over Rosie and then swung his Colt on the other two who were scrambling to arm themselves. The Gunsmith's weapon boomed four more times, and the other two men died falling out of their chairs, one still clutching a losing poker hand.

"Goddammit, Rosita," Clint swore in misery as he raced to her side. "I'm sorry!"

The first man he'd shot wasn't dead yet. Clint's bullet had plowed up through his backside and into his belly. He was going to die slow and hard, but Clint didn't care. He grabbed the man by the hair and hauled him off Rosie. Then, he pulled his hunting knife and cut the bonds that held Rosie spread-eagled across the bunk.

She sobbed and threw her arms around his neck, squeezing him hard. Clint let her cry for as long as she wanted. He held and rocked her like a child and he said things that he'd not said to a woman in a long, long time. Things that maybe made no sense, even, but that seemed to calm the brutalized half-breed girl.

When Rosita was finally composed, Clint said, "I'm going to drag those hunks of carrion outside and leave them to rot in the sun. Then I'll heat some water. You can have a bath and I'll cobble up something to eat. Rosita, you'll feel much better by daybreak."

"You came to take me to Mexico," she said, squeezing his hands. "You came to be my man!"

Clint wanted to say yes, but he couldn't. "Not exactly. I need a witness."

She was confused. "Witness?"

"Yes. I had to break out of jail in Butte City. They're charging me with one of the ambushes. Moss Taylor says that I shot the same gambler that loaned me his horse. He said it happened after we left Midan's village."

"That's not true!"

"I know that and so do you, but you have to come back to Butte City and tell the court."

"No! You come with me to Janos. We can be happy there."

"I'll come," he promised. "I'll take you to Mexico, and I'll stay a little while."

"Stay forever!"

"A little while, Rosita. Long enough to make sure that you are happy and will be well taken care of. But after that, well, I don't know."

"And if I don't do this 'witness'?"

Clint shrugged and said, "I'd take you to Janos anyway and then I'd come right back. I'm going to bring Moss Taylor down. One way or the other, I'm going to get that man and free the people of Butte City from his reign of murder and treachery. I owe that to John Lincoln and some of the other townspeople who have been good to me."

Rosita thought for a moment and then she said, "All right. I will be this 'witness' for you and then we will ride together to Mexico. Maybe when you see my village and the smiles of my people, you will stay longer than you think."

"Maybe," he said with a smile of relief.

EIGHTEEN

Clint wondered what kind of a state Butte City would be in when he and Rosita returned. No doubt his escape had caused quite a stir among the citizenry, and the Gunsmith was not exactly sure what to expect. It didn't seem prudent to just ride into Butte City and present Rosita as living proof that he had not been the one that ambushed John Lincoln. But really, what else was there to do?

Clint decided that he would sneak Rosita into town and then discuss his next move with Bud York and Thelma before he announced his return. Along with Doc Potter, they were his trusted friends and he valued their advice. And so, he waited until after dark and then he and Rosita rode through the dimly lit streets until they arrived at Bud's stable where they rode into the man's barn and dismounted.

Bud had constructed a small sleeping quarters in one corner of the barn. Clint approached it, hoping not to alarm Bud into taking him for a thief and perhaps shooting him in the semidarkness by mistake. "Hey, Bud! It's me, Clint Adams! Are you still awake?"

There was a rustling in the small room, and then Clint heard Thelma's giggles.

"We'll be right out!" Bud called.

Clint quickly unsaddled their weary horses and found them empty stalls. Not only did they have Duke and Rosita's pair of Indian ponies, but also the three mounts which had belonged to the cattle rustlers who had raped and abused Rosita. Clint figured that Bud would pay a fair price for those animals and their saddles, and the Gunsmith would split the money with the half-breed girl so they'd both have some travel money for Mexico—if he survived the showdown with Moss Taylor.

"Hello there!" Bud said, emerging from his sleeping room and tucking his shirt into his pants. He glanced at Rosita and even in the dim light of a hanging lantern, Clint could see that he was blushing with embarrassment. Thelma was still inside the sleeping room, probably getting dressed.

"Hello, Bud." Clint stifled a grin. "I'm real glad to hear that you and Thelma are getting along so well."

"Oh, we are for a fact!" Bud smiled broadly and lowered his voice so that Thelma could not overhear his words. "I took your advice about bathin' and usin' that perfumy stuff. Not too much though. Anyway, it sure did the trick. Thelma is crazy about me now. Today, I bought some new clothes and got a shave and a haircut."

"You look great," Clint said, meaning it. "I'm glad that things are working out so well between you."

Bud's face reflected pure joy. "I asked Thelma to

marry me tonight and she said yes!"

"Congratulations!"

Bud looked ready to bust his buttons. "I think I must be the happiest man in the world. We're going to get a house, and I'll hire a man to live here in my place. I'm going to start living like a respected citizen of Butte City. Maybe someday I'll even run for mayor."

"You'd make a fine mayor," Clint said, watching Thelma emerge with her hair a little mussed and her fine figure stretched tight under Bud's new shirt. "Evening, Thelma."

She smiled and slipped her hand through Bud York's arm. That told Clint that she wasn't angry because the Gunsmith was now with Rosita or that she'd had to settle for her second choice of a husband. The gesture gave him a great deal of satisfaction and the Gunsmith relaxed.

"Congratulations on your engagement, Thelma. I haven't a doubt in the world that Bud is going to make you a very, very happy woman and a proud mother."

Thelma stood a little taller. "Bud has always been a gentleman to me and when he's cleaned up, I think he's a real handsome catch."

"He is," Clint agreed. "Thelma, this is Señorita Rosita Lopez. She's the Ute medicine woman that healed my knee. Maybe just as importantly, she's a witness to the fact that I couldn't have ambushed John Lincoln."

Thelma stepped forward and stuck out her hand. "Welcome, Rosita. It took a lot of courage for you to come to Butte City and testify in Clint's behalf."

Rosita glanced at the Gunsmith with a question in her dark eyes, compelling Clint to say, "Thelma means that there are Indian haters in this town. People who mistrust the Utes because they have this crazy fear that Midan and his warriors are behind the full moon ambushes."

"This is not true."

"I know that and so do my friends, but you'll have to convince the others you are telling the truth."

"I can only say the truth. What they believe is up to them."

Clint looked to his friends. "The señorita doesn't quite understand how difficult it might be for her to convince the judge and . . ."

"Forget Judge Banes," Thelma interrupted. "I know the man, and he is totally corrupt. It wouldn't matter if John Lincoln were resurrected from the grave and came forward to say that Moss Taylor shot him—Judge Banes would still find you guilty of the crime and sentence you to hang."

"That bad, huh?"

"Yes," Thelma said. "There's only one way to win your case, and that's to take it right to the people."

"You mean call a town meeting or . . ."

"No, I mean we should march over to the Palace Saloon and tell everyone the truth. John Lincoln had a lot of friends there. He always ran a fair poker table, and he was respected. Tell the customers what really happened and who is behind the killings. Let Rosita talk."

"That's a big gamble," Clint said dubiously.

"At least the people will listen and try to make an honest judgment," Bud York argued. "Thelma and I are well-liked and respected. We'll stand or fall beside you, and our being there will make a difference."

"I'm sure it will," Clint said. "And it might not hurt to stop along the way and get Doc Potter."

"Good idea."

Clint looked at Rosita. "Are you willing to stand up in a saloon before a bunch of miners and rough men to tell them that I was with you when John Lincoln was killed?"

Rosita nodded her head very firmly.

"All right then," the Gunsmith said. "Let's get this over with."

They got Doc Potter, who had been about to retire for the evening. When he learned of their plans, the doctor dressed quickly and joined them on their march down the boardwalk toward the Palace Saloon. As they walked in a tight and determined body, the word seemed to flash up and down Main Street so that other men fell in behind them until there was a huge throng pushing its way into the Palace Saloon.

Clint held on tight to Rosita's hand. He could well imagine what a frightening experience this was for a girl who had never been in a white man's town and had known them only as her enemies.

"Everyone listen up!" he shouted, jumping onto the bar top and pulling Rosita up to his side where he held her close. "You all know me, but none of you know Señorita Rosita Lopez."

The crowd fell silent. One man, drunk and raucous, made some lewd remark but was quickly forced into silence by his curious partners.

"As you know," Clint continued, surveying the huge crowd that filled the interior of the saloon and spilled out the doorway, "I've been accused of ambushing John Lincoln. The motive given was that I just didn't want to pay him the price for losing his sorrel gelding."

Clint paused for a beat and then said, "I can tell you that's a barefaced lie."

"Can you prove it?" a big miner shouted.

"Yes! When John was ambushed, I was up at Midan's Ute camp negotiating a peace between his people and you folks. I asked the chief if he or any of his men had anything to do with the ambushings and Midan said no."

"What'd you expect that lying Indian to say?" another man shouted.

Clint held his temper. He could not afford to lose control now. "Midan understands that he can't aggravate the whites or his own few remaining people will taste your wrath and be exterminated."

"He's got that much right!"

Clint raised his hands for silence. "Midan and his few hungry people have had nothing to do with the ambushings—but the Utes told me who might."

Clint paused a moment, and the crowd hung waiting in breathless anticipation. "Do you want to know who the real ambusher is?"

"Hell yes!" the crowd roared as one voice.

Clint stared at them with more confidence than

AMBUSH MOON

he felt, because what he said next would determine if he lived or was hanged. "The real ambusher—whether he did the killings himself or had his gunmen carry them out—is Moss Taylor."

The crowd exploded with a mixture of shock and disbelief. Clint raised his hands and when he could not get silence, he drew his gun and fired two shots into the ceiling.

"Listen to me! It all makes sense when you think about it. Moss Taylor was present thirty years ago during the bloody battle between Old Chief Nacota, Benson, and the others. And it was Moss Taylor who lost a father and a brother. He has always sworn to get the Ute people and now he's come up with this ambushing business to incite you people into annihilating the last of the Ute people to satisfy his thirst for vengeance."

There was long silence, and then the crowd began to buzz. Finally, one voice rose about the others. "How do we know if any of what you're saying is true? You'd say any damn thing to keep your neck from being stretched."

Clint looked around. "There must be someone old enough to have been in Butte City thirty years ago during that fight."

"I was," Doc Potter said. "And though I'd forgotten, you're right. Moss Taylor was there and had the terrible trial of seeing his father and brother killed along with Chief Nacota and quite a few Utes."

"There!" Clint said. "You have a motive for the ambushings. Revenge! And what about Moss Taylor's claim that he saw me shoot John Lincoln?"

The Gunsmith squeezed Rosita's hand. "Tell them."

Rosita lifted her chin. She was pale, and Clint could feel her trembling, but she was determined. "This man was with me on the day that John Lincoln was shot. And what he had to say about Midan is also true. I know because I was there."

Clint waited for more words, but they did not come. Rosita had said her piece and saw no need to elaborate. Instead, she stood beside him, looking a little frightened but dignified and determined. Glancing at her from the corner of his eye, Clint felt an enormous sense of pride in this half-breed girl. No one who looked into her bruised but pretty face and heard her simple declaration could have failed to believe she was telling the truth.

Clint sensed the ground swell of support that filled the entire saloon. Men began to nod and some even smiled. The Gunsmith saw the respect in their faces.

"There's only one thing to do now," Clint said. "And that's to bring Moss Taylor to justice. I'm riding out to his ranch and I'd appreciate all the help I can . . ."

"Hold on!" Sheriff Denton called, bulling into the saloon with a double-barreled shotgun cradled in his fists. "Adams, you're under arrest!"

Before Clint could reply, a man stuck his leg out and tripped Denton to the floor, shouting, "This son of a bitch is in Taylor's back pocket the same as Judge Banes. You can bet they're all behind the ambushings of our friends. Let's teach the lying bastard a lesson!"

The crowd roared in agreement and fell upon Denton, kicking and beating him. Thelma cried out in protest and placed her hands over her eyes.

"Stay right here!" Clint said to Rosita a moment before he jumped off the bar top and tried to rescue the corrupt sheriff.

It was hopeless. By the time he did reach the fallen man, Denton had been stomped to death and was lying in a pool of blood.

One big miner said, "Abe Long was like a father to me. I guess justice has been served."

Clint knew that justice *had* been served. Sheriff Denton had tried to brain both Clint and Thelma, and he'd done it with a streak of sadistic pleasure. Now, he lay broken on a barroom floor. Someone yelled that Judge Banes was still in town, and a dozen men surged back outside to hunt up the poor man while Clint returned to lift Rosita down from the bar top. He would take her, Doc Potter, and Thelma to a safe place and then he'd join the crowd and go bring Moss Taylor down.

The crowd waited for Clint to resaddle Duke. Clint glanced over at Rosita, who would be staying with Thelma while he and Bud York carried out this last piece of hard business that would put Butte City to rest. Off to the east, the sun was rising over a range of peaks.

"All right," Clint shouted, "I'm taking command, and this will not be a lynch mob! We're going to arrest Moss Taylor and find an honest judge who will sentence him for his crimes!"

The crowd listened for a minute and then howled like a starving pack of wolves. And at that moment, Clint knew that men were going to die before many hours had passed.

NINETEEN

Moss Taylor's spread was called the T Bar Ranch, and it took better than an hour from the time that Clint rode across its western boundary until he spotted the huge, two-story ranch house. The moment that they were in view, about a half dozen T Bar gunmen began to gather in front of the wide veranda like a bunch of drones gathering about to protect their queen bee.

"Moss Taylor won't come peaceably," Bud predicted. "We're riding smack into a gun battle."

"I doubt that those six hired gunmen are stupid enough to be willing to take on the size of this crowd," Clint said, glancing around at the more than one hundred men who'd managed to get horses and join them. Behind the horsemen there were six or eight ore wagons filled with more miners. "I'm just hoping to avoid a slaughter."

"How are you going to handle this?" Doc Potter asked, clutching his medical kit and looking extremely worried.

"I don't know. I'll tell Moss Taylor that he's under arrest, and then we'll just see what happens."

179

"Arrest him on what charges?"

"Well," Clint said, "he lied when he had me arrested so let's call him on the cause of a false arrest."

"That charge won't hold," the doctor said. "Taylor's lawyer will get him free."

Clint supposed this was true. He didn't know exactly how he was going to prove that Moss Taylor was behind all the ambushings. All he knew for sure was that the vile old rancher was as guilty as sin.

When they entered the ranch yard, Moss Taylor emerged from his big house with a Winchester clenched in his fists. "That's far enough, Adams!" he bellowed. "You and all the rest turn around and git!"

"You're under arrest for the murder of John Lincoln!" Clint shouted as he drew Duke to a nervous standstill in front of the house.

Moss laughed. "You're not going to pin *your* charge of murdering John Lincoln on me! Where's your evidence?"

"I'll find it before the trial. I imagine that a few of your men might be willing to sing—if the price is right."

Moss's Adam's apple bobbed with mounting anxiety. "I should have expected that Sheriff Denton would fail and it would come down to a fight between the two of us."

Clint dismounted and handed his reins to Bud as he whispered under his breath, "If I fall, make sure that Moss chases me to hell."

Bud nodded. "If you go down, this might turn into a Civil War battle."

AMBUSH MOON

Clint stepped forward, aware that the six hired gunmen would love to take credit for ending his life.

"You boys stay out of this or you'll never live to see sundown," he warned.

The hired gunmen exchanged nervous glances. They looked past the Gunsmith to the huge and hostile crowd, and their hands moved far away from their guns.

One of them said, "We don't get paid enough to die. And it was him, not us, that ambushed all them fellas."

"Shut up!" Moss screamed. "Shut your lying mouth!"

Twenty feet from the veranda, Clint halted and his fingers splayed over his gun butt. "You're holding that rifle, Moss. Are you willing to bet that you can put a bullet into me before I can put one in you?"

"I am," the old rancher hissed, spittle flying from his mouth. "I'm going to put a bullet through your gut and watch you die whinin' for mercy."

"Is that the same rifle that you used to kill John Lincoln and all the others?"

"You'll never know."

"My guess," Clint said, "is that it's the very same. Only this time, you're going to have to shoot a man who's prepared to shoot right back."

"No problem."

Clint smiled coldly. "If your dead father and brother were as twisted and mean as you are, then I'm glad they died in that gunfight thirty years ago."

Something snapped in Moss Taylor. With a curse he whipped the rifle around. It was ready to fire, but the Gunsmith's first bullet shattered the breech as well as Moss Taylor's right hand. It tore off the rancher's trigger finger, and the old man howled in pain and tried to switch the rifle to his other side.

Clint's second bullet drove into the rancher's left knee and spun him completely around. Moss crashed over a chair and struggled to bring the rifle back to bear on Clint, but the Gunsmith kicked it from his grasp. The rifle went skidding across the porch.

"How did you choose the ones to die?" Clint demanded as he glared down at the hateful old man. "What did they do to deserve being ambushed?"

"Go to hell!"

Clint cocked back the hammer of his gun and pointed it at Moss Taylor's right knee. "Right now, we've each got a limp. You answer me, or the hangman will have to carry you up to the gallows just to put the noose around your neck."

"They were my enemies!" Moss screamed. "They all realized I was the ambusher and they tried to stop me!"

"And so you shot them one by one. You probably didn't even realize that each time you killed there was a full moon. But after a couple of ambushings, someone in town seized on the coincidence and made a big deal out of it and then jumped to the further conclusion that it had something to do with the Utes."

"Shoot me, gawddamn you! Finish this off!"

"Uh-uh," Clint said, holstering his gun. "You're going to trial. I wouldn't want to rob these folks of their invitation to a well-deserved necktie party."

To make sure that the mob did not stomp and kick the old man to death as they had the sheriff, Clint and Bud kept guard over him while Doc Potter bound up the rancher's wounds. He was tossed into a wagon and driven back to Butte City with the townspeople whooping and laughing and singing all the way.

"Bud," Clint said when they had Moss Taylor in jail, "how would you like to become the sheriff until this trial thing is over?"

"Well, I don't know."

"If you stand in as sheriff," Clint said, "the townsfolk won't forget that you rose to the occasion when needed. My bet is that it would make you a sure thing for mayor."

"It would?"

"Sure enough."

"Then I'll do 'er!"

Clint turned to Thelma. "Good-bye."

"You're not staying for the trial and hanging?"

"Nope," Clint said. "I'm bound for Old Mexico."

"With the girl. She loves you."

Clint chuckled. "By the time we reach her little village, I imagine she'll have had her fill of me and my headstrong ways."

Thelma's expression said that she didn't believe a word of it. Her eyes misted and she said, "I was hoping that you'd also be here for our wedding."

"I can't," the Gunsmith said with genuine regret. "I promised Rosita that, if she helped me out here and told the truth, I'd repay her the favor of an escort to Mexico."

"But if she waited a few weeks, the trial would be over and . . ."

Clint shook his head. "Thelma, that girl has already been waiting years to go back home. I've got to take her and I've got to do it now."

Thelma hugged his neck and whispered so that he alone could hear her say, "After Bud, I'll always love you."

"Thanks," he said, feeling his own throat tighten with emotion. "So long, Bud!"

"So long."

The Gunsmith went outside and headed for the livery, sure that's where he'd find Rosita anxiously waiting. And as he walked, people called his name and patted his back with congratulations.

Clint smiled, and his mind created a soft vision of a hammock and a glass of tequila and Rosita gently fanning a cool breeze across his face to the music of a Mexican guitar.

Watch for

SPANISH GOLD

149th novel in the exciting GUNSMITH series from Jove

Coming in May!

If you enjoyed this book, subscribe now and get...

TWO FREE

A $7.00 VALUE–

If you would like to read more of the very best, most exciting, adventurous, action-packed Westerns being published today, you'll want to subscribe to True Value's Western Home Subscription Service.

Each month the editors of True Value will select the 6 very best Westerns from America's leading publishers for special readers like you. You'll be able to preview these new titles as soon as they are published, *FREE* for ten days with no obligation!

TWO FREE BOOKS

When you subscribe, we'll send you your first month's shipment of the newest and best 6 Westerns for you to preview. With your first shipment, two of these books will be yours as our introductory gift to you absolutely *FREE* (a $7.00 value), regardless of what you decide to do. If you like them, as much as we think you will, keep all six books but pay for just 4 at the low subscriber rate of just $2.75 each. If you decide to return them, keep 2 of the titles as our gift. No obligation.

Special Subscriber Savings

When you become a True Value subscriber you'll save money several ways. First, all regular monthly selections will be billed at the low subscriber price of just $2.75 each. That's at least a savings of $4.50 each month below the publishers price. Second, there is never any shipping, handling or other hidden charges—*Free home delivery*. What's more there is no minimum number of books you must buy, you may return any selection for full credit and you can cancel your subscription at any time. A TRUE VALUE!

A special offer for people who enjoy reading the best Westerns published today.

WESTERNS!

NO OBLIGATION

Mail the coupon below

To start your subscription and receive 2 FREE WESTERNS, fill out the coupon below and mail it today. We'll send your first shipment which includes 2 FREE BOOKS as soon as we receive it.

Mail To: **True Value Home Subscription Services, Inc. P.O. Box 5235
120 Brighton Road, Clifton, New Jersey 07015-5235**

YES! I want to start reviewing the very best Westerns being published today. Send me my first shipment of 6 Westerns for me to preview FREE for 10 days. If I decide to keep them, I'll pay for just 4 of the books at the low subscriber price of $2.75 each; a total $11.00 (a $21.00 value). Then each month I'll receive the 6 newest and best Westerns to preview Free for 10 days. If I'm not satisfied I may return them within 10 days and owe nothing. Otherwise I'll be billed at the special low subscriber rate of $2.75 each; a total of $16.50 (at least a $21.00 value) and save $4.50 off the publishers price. There are never any shipping, handling or other hidden charges. I understand I am under no obligation to purchase any number of books and I can cancel my subscription at any time, no questions asked. In any case the 2 FREE books are mine to keep.

Name		
Street Address		Apt. No.
City	State	Zip Code
Telephone		
Signature		

(if under 18 parent or guardian must sign)

Terms and prices subject to change. Orders subject to acceptance by True Value Home Subscription Services, Inc.

11358-1

J. R. ROBERTS

THE GUNSMITH

_THE GUNSMITH #1: MACKLIN'S WOMEN	0-515-10145-1/$3.99
_THE GUNSMITH #132: THE GREAT RIVERBOAT RACE	0-515-10999-1/$3.99
_THE GUNSMITH #133: TWO GUNS FOR JUSTICE	0-515-11020-5/$3.99
_THE GUNSMITH #134: OUTLAW WOMEN	0-515-11045-0/$3.99
_THE GUNSMITH #135: THE LAST BOUNTY	0-515-11063-9/$3.99
_THE GUNSMITH #136: VALLEY MASSACRE	0-515-11084-1/$3.99
_THE GUNSMITH #137: NEVADA GUNS	0-515-11105-8/$3.99
_THE GUNSMITH #139: VIGILANTE HUNT	0-515-11138-4/$3.99
_THE GUNSMITH #140: SAMURAI HUNT	0-515-11168-6/$3.99
_THE GUNSMITH #141: GAMBLER'S BLOOD	0-515-11196-1/$3.99
_THE GUNSMITH #142: WYOMING JUSTICE	0-515-11218-6/$3.99
_GUNSMITH GIANT : TROUBLE IN TOMBSTONE	0-515-11222-7/$4.50
_THE GUNSMITH #143: GILA RIVER CROSSING	0-515-11240-2/$3.99
_THE GUNSMITH #144: WEST TEXAS SHOWDOWN	0-515-11257-7/$3.99
_THE GUNSMITH #145: GILLETT'S RANGERS	0-515-11285-2/$3.99
_THE GUNSMITH #146: RETURN TO DEADWOOD	0-515-11315-8/$3.99
_THE GUNSMITH #147: BLIND JUSTICE	0-515-11340-9/$3.99
_THE GUNSMITH #148: AMBUSH MOON	0-515-11358-1/$3.99
_THE GUNSMITH #149: SPANISH GOLD (May)	0-515-11377-8/$3.99

Payable in U.S. funds. No cash orders accepted. Postage & handling: $1.75 for one book, 75¢ for each additional. Maximum postage $5.50. Prices, postage and handling charges may change without notice. Visa, Amex, MasterCard call 1-800-788-6262, ext. 1, refer to ad # 206d

Or, check above books and send this order form to:
The Berkley Publishing Group
390 Murray Hill Pkwy., Dept. B
East Rutherford, NJ 07073

Bill my: ☐ Visa ☐ MasterCard ☐ Amex (expires)

Card#_____ ($15 minimum)

Signature_____

Please allow 6 weeks for delivery. Or enclosed is my: ☐ check ☐ money order

Name_____

Address_____

City_____

State/ZIP_____

Book Total $_____
Postage & Handling $_____
Applicable Sales Tax $_____
(NY, NJ, PA, CA, GST Can.)
Total Amount Due $_____